David Peak

The River Through the Trees

BLOOD BOUND BOOKS

ISBN 978-0-9849782-4-3

Artwork by M. Wayne Miller

Printed in the United States of America

First Edition

Visit us on the web at:
www.bloodboundbooks.net

Anthologies Available from Blood Bound Books:

Blood Rites: An Invitation to Horror

Night Terrors II

Rock 'N' Roll is Dead: Dark Tales Inspired by Music

D.O.A.: Extreme Horror Collection

Steamy Screams: Erotic Horror Anthology

Novels & Novellas:

The Sinner by K. Trap Jones

Sons of the Pope by Daniel O'Connor

Dolls by KJ Moore

Feeding Ambition by Lawrence Conquest

At the End of All Things by Stony Graves

Out—out are the lights—out all!

And, over each quivering form,

The curtain, a funeral pall,

Comes down with the rush of a storm,

And the angels, all pallid and wan,

Uprising, unveiling, affirm

That play is the tragedy "Man,"

And its hero the Conqueror Worm.

Edgar Allan Poe

"The Conqueror Worm"

Day One

1

Early Morning, Heavy Snowfall

Dan Robertson leaned over his desk with his face buried in the crook of his elbow, tired as shit from a thankless morning spent righting toppled tombstones. Just as he felt himself falling asleep, he heard the rude blast of a truck horn halfway down the cemetery driveway.

Through the icy panes of the window, he could make out the chrome grill of a Dodge Ram pickup as it came skidding to a halt in the parking lot. Tom Lucas.

Fuck.

He grabbed his Carhartt jacket from the coat hanger next to the door, put it on, and went outside.

Nearly a foot of fresh snow had piled up since Dan got to work that morning, sometime around six. He looked up into the silver swirl of the thickening sky.

Tom Lucas got out of his truck and slammed the door, then made his way over to Dan. He wore brown work pants over legs as thick as tree trunks. His face was red, his jaw square and shadowed with stubble. He wore the same kind of Carhartt jacket and Timberland work boots as Dan with a black Caterpillar skullcap pulled down just above his eyes.

The wind blew the falling snowflakes in erratic patterns. Tom walked with his face down and his eyes squinted. Snow crunched beneath his boots.

Sammy Veen and Bill Peterson cramped together in the Ram's cab, passenger side, almost sitting on top of one another, shoulders overlapping, identical with their thick beards and shaggy hair.

"What's going on, Tom?" Dan said, zipping up his jacket, breath visible. He rubbed his hands together, brought them up to his face and blew into them.

"How's it going, buddy?" Tom smiled and clapped him on the shoulder. He stood a full foot taller than Dan and was almost twice as wide. He was a monster. "Your sister come around?"

"Grace? She dropped me off this morning. Why?"

Tom's smile somehow stayed in place but his eyes went cold. He cracked his knuckles, turned his head at an angle, then back the other way, searching Dan's face.

The thin bones in Dan's hands already ached. It was so fucking cold.

"We got some work to do. Your sister said you could help us out." Tom smiled again. "Now why don't you just hop in the cab?" His voice was soft, restrained, like he was trying to coo a scared dog out from under the porch. "There's no need for any bullshit, Robertson."

Dan thought of the size of Tom's hands, the strength in his arms, all the beatings he'd taken from him as a kid, the years of bullying, the name-calling, the thing with Melissa Vanderzane—

"All right, I'll go."

"Good man." Tom clapped Dan on the shoulder once more before walking back to his truck.

"Oh yeah," he said, popping open the door, raising his voice over the wind, "go inside and get a tarp or a blanket or something." He climbed inside the cab.

Asshole. Dan walked back to the office, a small, one-room building done up to look like a log cabin. Inside, he went to the supply closet by the windows. He took out the blue plastic tarp they put over freshly dug graves in rainy weather. Out of the desk's top drawer he grabbed a handful of five-inch stakes, rusted through, old. Next thing he was back outside and climbing into Tom Lucas's truck.

The four men sat cramped in the cab of the Ram. Dan sat behind the passenger seat with his back up against the small window and his legs stretched across the seat. Bill and Sammy piled on top of one another next to Tom.

No one spoke as the truck bounced along the slippery, uneven dirt roads winding through the Northwestern Michigan woods. The heat blasted. The air in the cab reeked of cigarettes and stale coffee. Johnny Cash played through the speakers.

"So, how's your sister doing?" Tom said, eyeballing Dan in the rearview mirror.

"Half-sister. And she's fine."

"Still married to Fox?" Sammy said over his shoulder.

"Got a divorce when he got sent up. Never thought he was gonna give it to her, but he did."

"Go figure," Bill said. Dan could barely hear him over the noise of the air vents, the Cash. He felt his lips chapping, drying out.

"Ain't he supposed to be getting out soon?" Sammy said.

"Any day now," Dan said.

"She's the one that gives you rides to work, huh?" Tom said. "Grace, I mean."

"Yeah."

"Surprised you can't ride *her*," Bill said. The two of them, Bill and Dan, made eye contact in the mirror. Bill had been Dan's childhood friend, his best friend, had been there for him through the worst of it. Through all the shit with Bicycle Bob, with Grace. His cuts hurt worst. But that's what happens when people go weird, when something unthinkable happens and a person shuts up inside himself. Their best friends pretend like they never knew them from Adam.

"What?"

"Grace. Your sister. I'm surprised you can't ride her to work. I mean she *is* the town bicycle."

Dan felt his face flushing. That familiar itch.

"Oh, take it easy, Danny, you apple-faced faggot," Tom said. "Just a little light-hearted teasing. It's not your fault your sister's a freak."

Ten minutes or so burned by.

"How far along is it?" Dan asked.

"Not much," Tom said, hands wrapped around the wheel, body slack in his seat. And then, as if to nip any further conversation in the bud, he reached out and turned up the volume of the cassette deck.

Dan stared out the window. All he saw was snow, falling heavier now, clumps clinging to the claws of the leafless trees whisking by his window, gray blurs, whipping. There was nothing to focus on. *Maybe try to get a little rest.* He closed his eyes and immediately felt himself fall away. The mouth-warm air pumping out the vents enveloped him.

All around the truck the looming trees rushed by. In the old fairy tales they always told the little ones to stay out of the woods. Maybe it was true. Maybe things would be different for him, for Grace, if they had. But what could you do when the woods were everywhere?

Dan—he went by Daniel back then—and Bill were ten when they saw him for the first time. They were camping out on the land behind Bill's house. They were the first ones to see Bicycle Bob in the woods.

They had the fire going big and bright for twenty or thirty minutes, yellow crackling flames tall as the boys themselves. Everything beyond the light was black: the sky, the woods. They made camp in the clearing back by the deer meadows where Bill's dad put the salt licks, his family's property, running all the way to Silver Creek before it turned county.

Daniel sat in his folding chair with a huge can of baked beans between his legs, his face glowing in the firelight. He had his Swiss Army knife stuck straight down in the lip of the can, holding it in his fist, and he was sawing away, up and down, up and down, the blade screeching on the tin. It was a terrible sound, the kind of sound you felt in your teeth. Bill glared at him, and Daniel pretended not to notice.

Bill stood on the other side of the fire, poking at it with a blackened stick, getting at those glowing red embers deep inside, the ones that swelled like little beating hearts.

And even with that fire roaring, they still heard that asshole coming from fifty feet out. Branches snapping, twigs cracking, dead leaves shuffling. He trudged through those woods like a rhino—drawn to the fire, ready to stomp it out.

"You hear that?" Bill said.

Daniel's knife stopped, that terrible nerve-shredding noise stopped. He looked up, eyes wide. "Hear what?"

"That."

Another twig snapped, some leaves ruffled. He was closer now, that crazy fuck. Ten feet away. Hidden somewhere out in all that darkness, it seemed like the noise of his trudging came from every direction at once.

Then Bicycle Bob stepped out of the shadows.

He stopped and he stared, his sweat-slicked gut glistening and orange in the light of the fire. His belly button was deep, his chest sagged heavy, and his hair was done up like the Demon from KISS, big shocks of it on the sides of his head and a tight samurai-bun on top.

Dan would swear by it in the years to come, that Bicycle Bob had looked exactly like a bloated version of the demonic face that had spooked him so bad when he caught a glimpse of it in a rock magazine, that horrible blood-dripping mouth and the freakish tongue.

Bicycle Bob grumbled something unintelligible over the sound of the crackling flames, giggling and whispering. His fat lips rolled and flapped. He looked at Daniel, then back to Bill, his eyes black and gleaming like polished stones.

His face was white with pancake makeup, but either the heat from the fire or all that woods-stomping had made sweat carve through that powder and greasepaint, made it look like his face was melting right off, his black lips pointing downward in an unreal frown.

Then he turned around and stomped back into the black forest. Dan never felt right in the woods after that.

The legend grew from there: some fat freak was stomping around the woods done up like the bassist from KISS. It scared the shit out of every kid in town, gave every concerned parent an inarguable reason to toss out any KISS or Black Sabbath or Judas Priest album their kids might have smuggled into their bedrooms. He was stealing kids, everyone said. Taking them down to that big sewer grate at the end of Silver Creek, the reservoir, the one that collected the runoff from the storm drains, that fed the water treatment plant outside of town. The same place where Bicycle Bob took Dan's six-year-old sister, Grace. Where he changed her forever.

Dan didn't grow out of his fear of the woods and the dark. He grew into it. And now and again a stand of trees across a clearing looked to him like molars in the back of an open, screaming mouth.

Some said that Bicycle Bob wasn't even a real person, really. That his spirit traveled from one host to the next, corrupting that thing that made children pure, turning them evil. Or that he was Lucifer or the Devil or whatever people called him. The goat in a man's skin. The Bornless One.

And that's what still scared Dan. Just thinking about that white dripping face with the frowning, black-lipstick mouth. And what might be in the dark beyond his vision, or lurking beneath the dirty water of the Thornapple River.

The truck's door slammed.

Dan came to in the silence of the empty cab, slumped in the seat, neck aching, jaw sore as if he'd been grinding his teeth. The light was overcast, gray.

He rubbed the back of his neck, could hear the muffled voices of Tom, Bill and Sammy.

Dan went outside, looked around, did his best to see through the snowfall. He held the tarp under his arm. The Thornapple River raged everywhere all at once.

They were in a huge clearing in the woods. Dan recognized it as a popular boat launch, popular in the summer, at least. One large, hulking tree had grown close to the bank of the river, its branches reaching toward the sky. Its roots were wild and gnarled ropes.

Dan recognized Kenneth Thompkins's black Jeep parked back by the side of the road, sitting high on monster 4x4s.

Tom, Sammy, and Bill stood smoking cigarettes, facing the river.

"...the fuck we supposed to do?" Bill said, catching Dan with his eyes and elbowing Tom in the ribs.

Tom turned. Big smile. He threw his cigarette at the river. Bill and Sammy did too. "Let's show you where Thompkins bit the bullet."

"What?"

"Just move," Tom said. "We figured we'd come out here and get you, you know, to help us pick up the body. You get paid for that, right?"

Dan nodded. The county gave him a little bit of money for every deceased person he retrieved. But not like this. He had a gurney and a beat-up-but-still-running county van. He took them to the morgue in Forest View Hospital, or to the funeral home. He didn't cruise out in a pickup.

The four of them walked down to the bank. The river was all noise. Dan could barely hear Tom's voice over the roar. "Over here," he was saying, pointing to the large tree with the rope-like roots. "Behind the tree."

Dan didn't quite know what he expected to see. His guts felt all tight and hot. He'd long ago grown accustomed to being with the dead; he'd helped load up nearly a dozen corpses from all over town, usually with the Bazynski kid who worked for him in the summers. But this was different somehow.

Rounding the tree, the sound of the river faded away. The snow seemed to stop falling, just hung in the air, stuck in stillness.

A layer of frosty ice covered Kenneth's body. The tips of his work boots, toes pointing upward, were capped with snow. Dan could barely make out the red of his flannel shirt. Flecks of brown blood clung scattershot to the base of the tree.

The sound of the water came rushing back, louder now, and Dan—a feeling of vertigo, a push and a pull, passing through his chest in a wave—realized he was staring at the body of someone he had known, whose laugh he could pick out of a crowd.

Dan steadied himself against the tree with one hand, feeling light-headed. He shut his eyes and took a deep breath. Was Tom trying to say something to him? He didn't know. He couldn't hear anything. He swallowed his spit, opened his eyes and saw something stuck to the tree. Like a fungus, or a pale slug. Dan looked closer. It was a bit of Kenneth's brain. Small flecks of skull.

He stumbled a bit.

Tom's thick arms caught him and pulled him up. "Whoa there." Mock excitement. "What, you ain't used to this sort of thing by now? I thought this was part of your job."

"I'm sorry, I guess I just didn't expect…" Jesus, why was he apologizing?

"You see—" Tom paused. He was thinking. Then he was talking. "Blew his brains out last night with a .357, right here."

Dan didn't say anything, just shook his head. What was he supposed to say? There was nothing he could say.

"We found him 'bout a half hour ago, getting ready to do some fishing."

"Fishing now? It's freezing."

"Never too cold to fish, right." It wasn't a question. Sammy narrowed his eyes, pointed a finger at the tarp tucked under Dan's arm. "Look, just get him loaded up and we'll be done."

Dan swallowed hard, nodded. He went back to the body, laid out the tarp. From the pocket of his jacket he took out one of the old rusty stakes, staring at it for a few seconds before realizing that he wouldn't be able to get it through the frozen ground, not with his bare hands anyways.

"You got a hammer or something?"

He heard someone opening and closing the Ram's door. All that time, he kept his eyes on his hands, didn't know what else to do, what else to look at. And then Sammy was there, standing over him. He held the blade of a hatchet, handle extended toward Dan. "Just use the backside of the blade," he said, his voice buried beneath the rush of the water. Dan hammered in all of the stakes, clinking away with the hatchet, the sound muffled and soft, making sure that the tarp was secure in the wind.

Bill shook his head. "Why you covering him up? Thought you were gonna move him."

Dan pretended not to hear, then asked, "Where's the gun?"

"Where's what?" Sammy said.

"The gun." He felt his voice raising. "The gun. You said he used a Magnum. Where is it?"

"You seen how heavy it's been snowing? That gun's buried somewhere."

"Did you go to the police?" Dan asked.

11

Tom's chapped lips cracked open, made something like a smile, showed the quarter-sized gap between his front teeth. "Of course we went there first, dummy."

"And?"

"And no one was there."

"Call 'em?"

"You tried using your phone this morning? Jesus Christ, Robertson. The lines are down. Snow's been falling heavy the past few hours. Now why the fuck are you asking me all these stupid questions?"

The men stood in silence. Dan felt his heart beating beneath his heavy jacket, blood coursing through his neck.

"I can't move him without the cops here. I'm sorry, but I just—" The blood was hot beneath Dan's cheeks. Itching. Jesus. "It's fucking freezing out here, I can't just stand around waiting. Who's on duty today? Tupper? When's he getting here?"

"You'll be fine, man," Tom said. That smile. "This is Michigan, boy. Toughen up. You wait here. Right here."

The three men tramped away. Dan watched them disappear beyond the drifted slope beside the road. It was only after Tom gunned the engine and peeled off down the road back toward town that Dan realized he hadn't seen any fishing equipment in the truck. The snow fell thick all around him and the river raged ice-cold and all he could think about was how there were no poles, no tackle boxes, no nothing. And damn, if the gun had been buried under the snow all that time, how had Tom known its caliber?

2

Morning, Heavy Snowfall

That old familiar fear set in when Dan heard, or thought he heard, a peal of laughter coming from the woods. From all of the woods, everywhere surrounding the boat launch. It filled his head with phantom sounds, backward whispers and a chant like something from a Satanic horror film. But when he tried to listen, struggled to hear, there was only the beastly churn of the river.

"Fuck this," he said, scanning the tree line once again, snowflakes stuck to his eyelashes. Nothing to be seen beyond the shadows, everything obscured by the wash of white. He walked in place a bit, trying to stay warm, stuffed his hands in the pockets of his jacket.

A particularly nasty gust of wind made his head feel like it was splitting up the middle, loosened a corner of the tarp over Kenneth's body, snapping it back.

The boat launch had never felt so small, almost as if the woods were closing in. And then, crystal clear, the shrill sound of a bicycle bell—no mistaking it. Whatever was happening, whatever Dan was doing there with Kenneth's body, none of it mattered anymore. He had to get away, had to get back to town. Without even thinking, he was back at the road. If he was lucky he could hitch a ride back to town.

The Ram's tire tracks had almost completely disappeared beneath the heavy snowfall. A white curtain. Dan's head ached from the cold.

He stood by the side of the road for ten or fifteen minutes, shifting his weight from one foot to the other, before he heard the rip of a bad muffler. A small black Tercel came into view. He knew that car. Nancy Van Horton. He took a step into the road and waved.

The Tercel slid a bit in the snow as it pulled over. Dan opened the door and got in.

"Daniel Robertson. Gracious. What are you doing out here in this cold?"

"It's a long story." Dan rubbed his hands together. He was shaking bad.

Nancy was a small woman in her mid-fifties, with platinum-blonde hair done up in curls, eyebrows drawn on with pencil. She wore a knee-length fuchsia coat with imitation fur lining the hood. Her lipstick matched her coat.

"Sorry the heat don't work," Nancy said. "This car's a piece of shit."

"No matter, anything's better than out there."

Nancy put the car into first gear, popped the clutch and gave it some gas. Dan jerked back in his seat as the car took off.

"So where you going?"

"Town. Can you drop me off on Main?"

"You going to the post office?"

"Police station."

"Oh. Something the matter?"

14

Dan thought for a second. Thought against what he was thinking. "No, there's no matter."

The front-wheel-drive compact fishtailed as it climbed and descended the steep hills of the backcountry roads. The dash vibrated whenever Nancy hit the gas. The sound of the muffler tore into the soft spaces in Dan's head. The echo of the bicycle bell rang in his memory.

"So how's Kenneth doing?" Nancy asked.

Dan felt his heart skip a beat. "Kenneth?"

"I saw his Jeep parked back there—by the side of the road—thought maybe you and him were doing some fishing."

The Jeep.

"Kenneth's—"

"That man's gotta take hold of his life, you tell 'em that for me," Nancy said. "I been teaching at that school for going on thirty-seven years now and I've never encountered kids as ill-behaved and ill-mannered as his. You know, in his math class, Kenneth Jr. actually carved something into his arm with the needle of his compass."

Dan didn't know how to tell her that the man she was talking about, whose kids she was talking about, was dead, his brains sprayed across the snow, only two miles back.

"*Slayer.* That's what he carved. A heavy metal band. Bleeding like crazy. Plus," Nancy continued, her voice quiet, a whisper, "if you ask me, I think he had a bit of a problem with—" she clucked her tongue on the roof of her mouth, "—with the meth."

Dan stared at the floor between his feet. He touched the toes of his Timberlands together.

15

Nancy shrugged. "I mean, what do you do with kids who cut themselves open in school?" Her voice went natural again, sounding regular, at ease. "He was seeing your sister for a while wasn't he? Kenneth, I mean." Nancy rubbed some frost from the windshield.

"Maybe back in high school. I can't remember." A pause. "She's just my half-sister."

"She still married to Fox?"

"Divorce."

Nancy put the car in third and started gunning it up a steep hill.

Nancy was quiet. She wasn't going to ask what Fox got sent up for. She already knew. Didn't everyone know? Then, in a confiding voice, "Everyone's going to hell around here. You noticed that?" Another pause. When she spoke again, her voice was cheerful, warm. "And your mom? How's your mom doing?"

"Not so great."

Nancy turned and looked Dan in the eyes. "That's a shame, sweetie. It's always the good ones, ain't it? You give her my regards, will ya?"

"Sure, I'll tell her."

Dan felt a heavy weight press behind his eyes. He pinched the bridge of his nose with his thumb and his index finger. A pressure was building up, threatening to spill over.

"You all right, honey? Just let it all out. There's some Kleenex in the glove box. You shouldn't be wiping your eyes with your sleeves like that. I didn't mean to upset you. Oh, Jesus. It'll all be okay, you'll see."

16

~

Nancy dropped Dan off in front of the police station. As he climbed out of the car she said, "Make sure you say hi to your mom for me, now. And try to take care of yourself. Get some rest, sweetie."

Dan shut the door and waved her off. He'd never been so embarrassed, a grown man crying in front of a woman. Fuck's sake, she'd been his ninth-grade teacher. He watched as the Tercel reached the corner and stopped. Nancy beeped the horn a few times, turned the corner, and disappeared behind the police station's red brick walls.

The station was a single-story building. An American flag flapped like crazy on a metal pole placed in the icy yard.

He saw his reflection in the glass doors. He looked like shit. His shoes were caked in frozen mud. Jagged white salt stains spiked up his pant legs.

He looked old.

Dan pushed the doors open and entered the building.

The air in the lobby was dry. The heat was cranked way up. He ran his tongue over his lower lip, chapped bad, split up the middle and stinging. A few wooden chairs were lined against the wall. Behind a large desk, behind a sliding glass panel, sat Derrick Tupper. Dan knew Derrick's older brother Rob. They'd been on the bowling team together in high school. Rob was one of the nice guys. But most of those guys went to college. You never heard from those guys again. The world out there welcomed them.

Dan approached the desk. His boots, wet from the snow, squeaked on the linoleum.

Derrick was young, clean-cut. He had pale eyes and a red complexion. His hair was cropped close to his skull and his uniform was cleanly pressed, dark blue, badge gleaming under the lights. He slid open the glass panel and smiled. "Dan Robertson. What can I do you for?"

Dan didn't know what to say, where to start. His head was all screwed up. He thought he might start crying again, maybe, or maybe not. He didn't know. He couldn't think. "Is there someone I can talk to? You know, if something..." he struggled to find the right words. "Look, I know where there's a dead body."

"A dead body? Whose?" A straight line creased in the center of Derrick's forehead. He looked down at the desk. "Whoa, that's a weird thing to say."

"There was an accident."

"What kind of an accident? Be specific."

There was no way getting around it. He was going to have to come out with it. So he told Derrick everything he knew, everything that had happened. And then, "Tom told me it happened last ni—"

"Tom? Tom *Lucas*?"

"The dumb fucker himself. Look, can I jus' sit down with someone and explain the whole thing in one swoop? I don't want to hafta go over it again and again."

"Yeah," Derrick said, lurching out of his chair, sending it swiveling. He popped out a door along the side of the desk. "Follow me."

18

Derrick led Dan down a long hallway of countless closed doors and low lights.

They came to an unmarked door. Derrick swung it open, a small room with white walls and no windows, and in its center was a gray table surrounded by three chairs.

"Take a seat," Derrick said.

Dan heard the door shut behind him as he sat down and leaned forward over the table, resting. *Say hi to your mom for me, now,* Nancy had said. He shook his head. His mother's mind had gone years ago. He sat in the white box of a room, trying to think of nothing at all.

Daniel's mother had shoved him face down on the hard wood floor, her left knee pressed into the crook of his neck, tendons pulled tight. He squirmed, strained, teeth clenched. His legs thrashed. The thud of his knees hitting the floor.

"Ma," he said, "get off. Get off me. You're hurtin' me."

She ignored him, dug her knee in harder, held him down tighter.

A lamp in the corner of the room glowed warmly. It was nighttime, windows obsidian.

"This is for your own good, boy," she said. "Now hold still." She held a sewing needle in her mouth like a cigarette and her words were all muffled.

She tightened her grip, staring down at the jagged gash arching over the bulge of Daniel's shoulder. It was a nasty cut, folded flesh-flaps on either side, skin puckered.

Bright red blood stained the skin around the cut but, somehow, Daniel had stopped bleeding before he'd come home. The resiliency of a youthful body.

Daniel's tears and spit spattered the floor. She applied more pressure to his neck.

Moving quickly, she released her left hand, snatched up the spool of fishing line and removed the needle from between her lips.

"Hold still now." She shifted her weight, using her knee to pin Daniel's forearm to the ground.

She let go of Daniel's bicep and skillfully threaded the needle with the fishing line. She tied the line into a knot around the needle's eye and gave it a tug. The line went taut, made a thick twang.

"This is gonna hurt," Bessie said. She bit down on the tip of her tongue, concentrating. "This is gonna hurt bad but you need to bear through it. Close your eyes." She meant for her voice to sound soothing. It came out anything but. "Don't think about the pain."

She lowered the tip of the needle to the gash on Daniel's shoulder, pressed the tip into the surface of the skin, felt it slide through, heard a dull snapping noise.

Daniel's knees thudded the floor. But he took it without squealing, without complaint. Like a little man.

Bessie pulled the fishing line through the flap of skin, gave herself a foot or two of line to work with. It was going to take a lot of slack to get through this cut, that was for sure.

She slipped the needle through the underside of the skin and pulled the line through. At the tip of the wound,

Bessie held the gash together with her thumb and index finger, doing her best to make sure that the cut would heal up evenly. She reversed her threading, pulled it through once more, reversed it again, continued.

The boy went silent, his body rigid.

Crickets chirped in the fields outside, filling the darkness beyond those black-stone windows.

And then she climbed up off her son to get a pair of scissors.

Freed of his mother's weight, Daniel didn't move. He just laid there, arms at his sides, breathing hard.

He fell asleep like that—belly-down on the floor— before Bessie returned with the scissors to cut the line from the spool. The stains of blood on his arm and shoulder had hardened into a crust. For a second, Bessie toyed with the idea of getting the alcohol out from beneath the bathroom sink. That gash was grisly; it could get infected. But Daniel had been through enough for one day. In the morning, she'd wash him up, dab some cotton balls in the alcohol and clean out all that dirt and dried blood. In the morning.

She picked her son up off the floor and carried him up the stairs to his room. He hung from her arms, head and feet dangling. He was getting heavy and pretty soon she wouldn't even be able to lift him anymore. His mouth hung open. He snored. His breath was sweet.

She put him down in his bed, turned off the light and went back downstairs to clean up, only then realizing that when Daniel had burst through that front door squealing and crying, he'd been alone.

His sister Grace was still missing, six years old and out there somewhere in that night, lost amongst the solid sound of the crickets and their terrible hum.

"Mr. Robertson?"

Dan looked up, groggy, disoriented. He'd fallen asleep. A man wearing a white button-up shirt and a skinny black tie stood before him. He had a handgun holstered on his hip.

"Mr. Robertson?" the man repeated.

"Yeah." Dan's voiced cracked. "I'm Mister." Jesus. He was nervous. Scared. Did he just say his name was *Mister*?

But the guy didn't seem to have noticed, or didn't mind, at least. "My name is Hapscomb, Mr. Robertson. I'm a detective."

Dan sat up in his chair and blinked a few times. This guy looked like he was in his early thirties, fit and healthy, muscular. His hair was black, eyes dark. He looked like someone you'd see on TV, someone selling dog food or razors. One of those guys who always looks like other guys, handsome but forgettable, interchangeable.

"I've never seen you before."

"They brought me in from Grand Rapids."

"Oh. Sweet arena you guys got there."

"Listen, you wanna take your coat off?"

"No."

Hapscomb sort of hesitated, like he was thrown off guard. "No? You sure? It's awfully hot in here."

Dan didn't want to get too comfortable, didn't want to believe that he was going to be in this room for a long time. For some reason, it made sense to him, keeping his coat on, made him feel as if he was on his way out. "I like my jacket to be worn," he said, and again, felt stupid because everything he was saying sounded so stupid. Because he was an idiot.

"Okay, sure." A brief pause. And then like a sudden movement, jarring. "Look, I'm not going to bother reading you your rights. I don't think I have to. We're dealing with a serious crime here and I need you to tell me what you know."

Dan fumbled to explain things, telling as much as he knew, letting the words fall out of his mouth, eventually getting into a rhythm, getting comfortable, giving context, details, feelings. He told the detective everything, well, almost everything. He left out the part about Tom mentioning Grace, but only because he hadn't worked out the connection yet. But other than that, he told him everything, because only guilty people didn't talk, right? Only guilty people had something to hide. Talking to a detective could never get you in trouble, not when you hadn't done anything wrong.

Hapscomb kept his head down, scratched notes into a small notepad.

When Dan finished, Hapscomb took a few moments to look over what he'd written. "Okay. Here's a question: Why did you go with them?" His voice was matter-of-fact, flat. He kept his eyes on the notepad.

Did detectives on TV look like they should be selling dog food in commercials? Now this guy looked like, Dan didn't know, like he shaved too much, like his skin was too smooth or something. Like one of the bad guys in a bad movie. One of those guys who did bad things for no reason at all.

"I didn't have a reason not to." It came out sounding like a question, his voice lilting. "I mean, there's no point in arguing with Tom."

"You and Mr. Lucas have a pre-existing relationship, you know, prior to today's events?"

"Well, yeah. Of course. We both grew up here, so."

"And this Mr. Lucas said that he had stopped by the station earlier in the morning—"

"That's correct."

Hapscomb's eyes were back to his notepad. He tapped his fingers along the edge of the table and pushed up from his chair. "Wait here just a minute." And then he was gone, left the room, door clicking shut softly behind him. And Dan was alone with his cheeks burning, like they were burning hot, like coming indoors to a hot room after being out in the cold snow all day. Why was he always saying such stupid things?

It was then, at that moment, that Dan started wishing he hadn't said anything at all. The right to remain silent. His blood raced. Fuck. He was such an idiot.

The detective came back a few minutes later. There was no expression on his face. Like he'd shaved any expression off. "Tom Lucas was never here. He lied to you."

24

Dan tried not to react. The detective watched him closely. He kept his face, what, slack or whatever.

"Look," Hapscomb said, "I believe that you're telling me the truth. I never read you your rights because I had no intention of arresting you. The same way you answered all of my questions, right? Because you had no fear of incriminating yourself."

Dan couldn't help but stare at the creases on Hapscomb's pants; they were perfect, almost like they were starched. Like a nerd's. And then, all those dudes from TV or whatever, they fell away, and Dan saw this detective as a real person, for the first time, and he realized that he was looking at a real-life detective. And that anything he said, everything he said, mattered. He couldn't help but feel like he was being fucked with.

"You, Mr. Robertson, are going to have to learn to trust me."

After that, Hapscomb swabbed Dan's thumb and index finger, explaining that he was going to test the results for gunshot residue. "Merely protocol," he said, dropping the swab into a small plastic bag. And then he left.

Five cups of water and three trips to the bathroom later, Derrick Tupper opened the door. "You ready to go, Dan?"

"I can leave?"

"That's right. Just got word from Hapscomb over the walkie-talkie, he says it's okay if you go back to work."

"What time is it?"

"'Bout twenty past noon. Damn, you must be roasting in here with your jacket on."

"Wait a second." Dan stood and stretched his arms out at his sides. "I don't have a car. You think maybe you can give me a ride out to the cemetery?"

"That's the plan."

3

Early Afternoon, Medium Snowfall

The middle between the haves and the have-nots had almost completely disappeared in these small towns. Hapscomb should know. He used to live in one.

But he was smart. He got out.

Back when he was a kid, it wasn't so bad; there used to be two of everything. Two lumber yards. Two drug stores. People had some spending money in their pockets. Everyone's fences were painted up nice every summer. Now there was only a big box store outside town, eating all the business.

Retired people. Rich farmers. Bankers and lawyers. They were doing all right. They had pensions, 401ks. They lived in the big houses up on the hills, away from the roads at the end of winding drives. But then there was everybody else. Around Hapscomb's office, they called them the "welfare dump." Low rents. Kids with learning problems, eating up all the funding. Shit was only going to get worse.

No. This place wasn't much different from any other small town. And it was damn depressing to see how things had changed. Or hadn't changed. After all, the class differences are all the same, all on the surface, breeding discomfort.

It will always be that way. The smartest students will leave; the best athletes will get scholarships. If you have a law degree, where are you gonna go practice? Here? A place like this?

Hapscomb's Crown Victoria slid to a halt where the icy road met the gentle slope of the boat launch. He got out of the car, ducked under the yellow tape flapping in the wind, and made his way down to the scene, dress shoes slipping with every step, socks already soaked.

The launch was crawling with plainclothes and uniforms alike. Flashbulbs bursting blue. Tightly clustered groups of men, breath shooting in the cold air, white-Styrofoam coffees steaming, beige overcoats, cigarettes. The tight laughter familiar to any investigation.

The river roared. A great wash of noise. Silver rushing sound.

Hapscomb made his way over to forensics. Hal Miller. Bent over what had to be the corpse at the base of a wildly gnarled tree, dark-barked, nearly black, branches like flexing muscles. Miller was brushing snow from the body, delicate-like, like the paleontologists in the movies, dusting off dinosaur bones. He wore a dark jacket. Police issue. Black pants, rubber boots.

"Miller," Hapscomb called out, raising his voice above the river. "Tell me what we got."

Hal looked back over his shoulder, face thin and long, chin jutting out. He saw Hapscomb and stood, crossing his arms over his chest.

"Always straight business with you, isn't it?"

Hapscomb shrugged and smiled.

"Can't you open up with a joke or something?"

"Just tell me what we got."

"All right then. How about I tell you what we don't got—a suicide."

"Homicide?"

"If I've ever seen one."

"Who's the victim?"

One of the uniforms handed Miller a cup of coffee. "Thank you," he said and took a long sip.

"Plate on the car up the hill is registered to a Kenneth Thompkins. Got his number out of the system and called his house—no answer. Guy's got two kids. Single dad. Called the school to see if we could get some ID but the receptionist says the kids haven't been in school for months. AWOL."

"The body covered in a tarp?"

"Yeah, it was. Some asshole—"

"Give me the rest of the details."

Miller didn't bat an eye. "Bullet exited through the back of the head, first thing. And, I'm only guessing here, but it looks like it went through upward, at a 45-degree angle, roughly. Autopsy will confirm it." He extended two fingers, hand in the shape of a gun. "Like this." He squatted down a foot or so, aiming upward, pointing his fingers into Hapscomb's face. "Bang."

"What else?"

"No murder weapon."

"Couldn't find it in the snow?"

"Not happening. The snow's already frozen into ice. Thing is, if it'd been a suicide, the gun woulda still been in

29

his hand. The muscles tense up, you know, during death, forms a helluva grip. But we got nothin'. Unless you want to rig up a generator and set up a system of heaters to melt the snow we're gonna have to wait until some of this ice thaws." Miller stomped his boot twice on the ground. "Like fucking rock."

"Shit," Hapscomb said.

"Plus, no tattooing on the face, no powder burns on the hands."

"Listen, I'll be in touch with you tonight. We've got other options." He handed Miller the small plastic bag with Roberston's residue swab. "Get this tested. It'll be clean, so don't bother calling me to tell me it's clean. But I want it tested all the same. Due diligence. All goes well we won't have to dig through any of this snow."

"Got it."

"Get this body out of the ice and get it to a morgue."

"There's a problem with that."

Hapscomb blinked. Waited for Hal to continue.

"Have you ever laughed before, Hapscomb? Told a joke?"

Hapscomb stayed silent.

Hal sighed. "You're impossible. Listen, Ardor doesn't have a medical examiner, an appointed official—a schoolteacher named Van Horton, guess she used to be a med student—but she's at work. No morgue, either. We're gonna have to ship the body one town over—they've got one at the hospital in Forest Hills."

"Have the examiner called in. I want ballistics on file as soon as possible, a full report."

"Okay—"

"No," Hapscomb interrupted. "Scratch that directive regarding the M.E. I'll go see her myself. I want to talk to her. Finish up here, report back to me. Got it?"

Hal frowned, exaggerating a military salute. "Yes, sir."

Back in his car, Hapscomb radioed to the station. Derrick picked up.

"Let Robertson go."

"You sure?"

"Yeah. Let him go." The man was innocent, Hapscomb knew that much. But sometimes, playing the innocent man like he was guilty was the best way to find out what he needed. When guilty people get comfortable, when they think someone else is going to take the heat, they start making mistakes. They do stupid things like talk too much, or return to crime scenes. This was a small town, after all. These people didn't say nothing bad about nobody, not to no outsider, because there was always that risk, that they might be talking shit to somebody's cousin or brother-in-law or best friend from high school from forever ago. "Give him a ride back to work. And put out an APB on William Peterson, Samuel Veen, and Thomas Lucas."

4

Afternoon, Light Snowfall

The gray-felt interior of Derrick's '89 Caprice was dusted with cigarette ash. Dan buckled his seatbelt and stretched out his legs.

Derrick kept his window all the way down and the heat all the way up, chain-smoked as he drove, ashing out the window. Wind whipped through the car as Derrick picked up speed.

"Looks like the snow is settling down, though," Derrick said. "Maybe they'll get the phones back up soon."

Dan looked out the window. The snowfall wasn't so thick anymore. Small flakes few and far between. The sky just as dull and gray as it had been all morning.

"Do you know what's going on out there by the boat launch? Or when I can get my tarp back?"

Derrick stopped at a red light. The car rattled and shook. The heat blasted, noise deafening. "Dan, you're probably not gonna ever get the tarp back. It's evidence now. And no, I don't know nothing more than you do."

The light turned green and Derrick gunned it. The back-end of the Caprice fishtailed from the left to the right before straightening out.

A little later they reached the foot of the cemetery driveway.

"Shit," Dan said.

"What?"

"Left the fucking gate open."

The car slid up the driveway and into the empty lot. Derrick parked diagonally across three spaces in front of the building.

Derrick turned off the car and unbuckled his seat belt. "You got a coffee maker in there?" He pointed to Dan's office.

"Yeah. What I made this morning's gone cold, but you want me to make a pot?"

Derrick rubbed his stomach with his right hand. "That all right with you?"

"It's fine, don't put me out or nothing."

"All right then," Derrick said, getting out of the car.

The snow in the parking lot had been packed down with boot prints, someone had been walking in circles. Dan felt his stomach tighten. *Somebody was here.* The prints led up to the door of the office.

Derrick walked up to the office door. "Well come on then, let's get that coffee on."

Dan slammed the car door shut and stuffed his hands into the pockets of his jacket. Wanted to be alone, wanted to get rid of this asshole. Sometimes, Dan just hated having to talk to people. It was the hardest thing in the world, to have to talk to other people when he got in one of his moods. Fucking painful.

"Who do you think was here?" Derrick asked.

Dan grunted.

"Can't argue with that," Derrick said, still smiling. His pale skin looked sallow, eyelids speckled with little purple veins. "Listen, if you don't put coffee inside me in about three minutes I'm going to just die. Feel like I've been awake for days."

Dan unclipped his keys from the belt loop of his pants, found the right key with his fingers. "Pardon me," he said, motioning to the door with the key.

Derrick took a step to the side.

Dan opened the door. There was a small sheet of paper on the floor of his office, folded over, with his name on it. Illegible almost. Pencil. Grace's handwriting. Dan snatched it up. He took a step into his office and, at the same time, stuffed the paper into his jacket pocket.

"Whad'ya take with your coffee?" he asked, walking to the small Mr. Coffee he kept by the sink in the back of the room.

Derrick shut the door behind him. "Lots of sugar." He stomped his boots against the welcome mat, stomping off the snow, the ice. "More sugar than you'd think was healthy. Like when you think you've put in as much as humanly possible, put in another pack or two."

Dan started the coffee maker. He looked around the room to see if anything else had changed. If there were any other signs that someone had been here. But everything was exactly how he had left it. All his papers were still on his desk. The shovels were still leaning up against the wall by the door, wastebasket still stuffed with fast-food wrappers.

"Grab a seat," Dan said. "I'm just gonna be a minute."

Derrick eyed a copy of *Field & Stream* on Dan's desk. "Take your time."

Dan squeezed himself into the tiny bathroom and shut the door. The toilet water had developed a thin layer of ice. He grabbed the grimy toilet brush and jabbed at the ice with the tip of its handle, didn't know how much Derrick could hear from out there, and decided to make his time in the bathroom sound as authentic as possible. He dropped his pants and sat on the toilet, cold; the seat bit into his hamstrings, but he barely felt it. His mind was on nothing except the note in his pocket, out of his pocket. He unfolded it, smoothed it out over his knee.

> *Dan,*
> *Was here looking for you around noon.*
> *Am in trouble. Need $. Do you have any you*
> *could give me? Maybe some of Bessies? I'll*
> *come back soon and try you again.*
> *Grace*

He reread the note several times, hoping each time that it would reveal something new. It didn't. All he knew for sure was that his sister had been here, at the cemetery, at the office. *If this is for drugs, I'm gonna tell her she's cut off.* But of course it was for drugs. What else would it be for? With Grace, one way or another, it was always about drugs.

Dan tore up the note and dropped the pieces into the water, flushed the toilet, left the bathroom.

Derrick was pouring a packet of sugar into his coffee. There was already a pile of empty sugar packets, their ends torn off, next to his cup. Sugar everywhere all over the counter. Kid was a slob.

"Everything all right?"

"Everything's fine. How's the coffee?"

Derrick slurped loud, turned around, leaned back against the counter. "French Roast? Jesus Christ. Stick a dick in my ass."

"That's just what my sister buys."

"Yeah, Grace." Derrick took another sip of his coffee. "She still married to Fox?"

"He got sent up."

Derrick raised his eyebrows. He took a long, annoying sip and said, "Dude, I'm a cop. I know he got sent up." He took another sip. "You know, I never could figure what she saw in a guy like Fox, anyways. Girls going for the grizzly-man survivalist type always baffle me. The way I see it, if you can't do something so simple as shave your face in the morning then how do you expect people to trust you with responsibilities?"

Dan poured himself a cup of coffee.

"Kenneth was seeing Grace for a while too, wasn't he?"

"Yeah. While back."

"Word is that Kenneth was selling drugs up at Fox's old cabin. The Newbert brothers made the connection for him. All sorts of stuff." Another slurp. "Grace ever talk to you about any of that?"

"Any of what?"

"The brothers. Drugs. Anything like that? You know, we get people coming in talking about all kinds of crazy shit that goes on up there on Bolt Street. Preston, you know he doesn't live too far from there? He says couple of his goats went missing last October. One of 'em was only a baby. Totally convinced that they got stolen for some sort of religious sacrifice."

Dan had heard all of these rumors before. They were as old as the town itself. He opened his mouth to say as much, but then he remembered how eager Derrick had been for a cup of coffee, how easily they'd let him go. All starting to make sense now. *They think I know something.*

"No. Grace never talked about any of that shit with me."

"Oh well, I guess—"

A car engine revving. Outside.

Derrick turned, looked out the window. "Who's that?"

Dan crossed the room and rubbed the icy windowpane with his sleeve, peered outside. Grace's rust-bit Corolla coming up the drive.

"Oh, shit. It's my sister."

Grace parked sideways behind Derrick's Caprice. She cut her engine and got out of her car, slammed the door. Her hair was greasy, Dan could make out that much from far away, her eyes dark in their sockets.

Not caring what Derrick might think, Dan opened the door and met her outside.

Grace's eyes went round. "Dan, I—"

"What are you doing here?"

Grace's face twisted. "I left you a note earlier, I—"

"Derrick Tupper is inside."

Grace's face went slack. "I saw the car." She looked exhausted. A big sore dotted the space between her eyes on her forehead. Her lips were peeling. "Come inside." He grabbed the sleeve of her denim jacket. "You look like shit."

Dan opened the door and led her inside.

Derrick was still leaning against the counter, arms crossed over his chest. "Howyadoin', Grace."

Grace stopped and stared at Derrick. Her face was sweaty, covered in a film of sweat, gleaming.

"You mean since the last time you made me spend the night in county?" She unwrapped her scarf from her neck. "I'm fucking fine."

Derrick laughed a high-pitched laugh and sipped his coffee.

"I don't mean to come off as a bitch," Grace continued, her hands on her hips, "but, you see, I'm here to see Dan. It's about our mother. She's sick. Did you not know that?"

Derrick shrugged his shoulders. "Family's family."

"If it's all right with you I'd like to take Dan home so he can look after his mother. Don't you lowlife assholes have some jaywalkers to fuck with your nightsticks? Or maybe you want to buy some more meth from me and then go squealing when you get caught with it? Fucking dumbass."

Dan sighed and stared at the ground. "Jesus Christ."

"You're a classy lady, Grace," Derrick said. He squinted. "Looks like your face is changing shape."

"All right now," Dan said. "Both of you—shut up."

Grace turned and put both hands on Dan's shoulders. Her face was mottled with red bumps; he noticed another open sore on her lip. She smelled like hairspray, cigarette smoke and sleep. "I'll tell you about it when we get in the car. Don't worry about it now."

"Well," Derrick said. "Thanks for the coffee, Robertson." He walked across the room and stopped in front of Grace, stared.

"Just 'cause you wear that uniform don't mean you're who you think you are," Grace said.

Derrick smiled, nodded at Dan, and left.

"So nothing's wrong with Mom?" Dan said, climbing back into Grace's car after he'd locked the gate. "You just made that up?"

"She has stomach cancer." Grace leaned over the wheel with her eyes squinted, trying to see through her mud-caked windshield. "I didn't make anything up."

Empty pop cans clattered in the backseat. The ashtray in the center console was filled with lipstick-stained butts.

"I know she has stomach cancer, God dammit. I fucking take care of her every day. But two minutes ago you said she'd taken a turn for the worse."

"I never said that. You just assumed that. I needed to get you away from rat-fucker."

"To ask me about money?"

Grace's voice went low. "Yes. To ask you about money."

"Well?" Dan put his back up against the car door and stared at his sister. She was biting her bottom lip raw.

"Well what?"

"What about money?"

39

"I need some."

"No shit. How much?"

She waited. And then, "Two thousand dollars."

Initially, he thought she was kidding. But she wasn't. He could see it on her face. Dan turned in his seat and stared out the window. "Why would you even think I have that much money?"

"Listen to me, your mom does, doesn't she? I said listen. Fox is getting out in a few days. I need that money. I can't go into why. Just trust me."

"I've told you this before but this time I mean it—you are cut off. Nothing ever again. I haven't even heard from you in—"

Grace's mascara was running down her face in clownish, purple streaks. Dan knew, from experience, that she only ever cried when she was frustrated, when she didn't get what she wanted. "You haven't even asked me what it's for." She floored the gas pedal, throwing Dan back into his seat.

"But you just said you wouldn't tell me."

Grace snapped on the blinker and turned the corner onto Kissing Rock Drive. The grill of a Dodge Ram pickup truck flashed as it approached from behind.

"Oh, shit." Dan dropped down in his seat.

"What?"

Dan turned in his seat and glanced out the rear window. Tom's Ram had stopped at the intersection. His right blinker was on. He wasn't moving.

Farther away now. Fifty feet. One-hundred feet. Tom's truck still wasn't moving. And then they were gone.

Grace turned the corner. The pavement ended and the road turned to dirt. The urban sprawl of the town faded into small, ugly houses, sleeping cornfields and endless rows of evergreens.

She parked the car on the side of the road and left the engine running. Bessie's tiny farmhouse was set back from the road. All of the curtains were pulled shut behind the windows.

"Why'd you duck down when Tom drove by?"

"Listen," Dan said. "Something happened to—"

"Can I have some fucking money, or what?" And there it was. That familiar ferociousness. Grace had once again revealed herself, as she always did.

"I already told you. The answer's no."

"What if I told you the money was for Amway?"

Dan couldn't help but laugh. A long-running joke. Every time Grace borrowed money, she'd say she was gonna use it get rich selling Amway. And for a second, that flash of humor, Dan saw all the good things in his sister. Half-sister. Whatever. Her softness. Her pain. His voice, his voice was gentle when he spoke. "When's the last time you saw your daughter, Grace?"

She stared at her hands clasped around the steering wheel. She had a small, jagged cross tattooed above one of her knuckles. A tiny goat's eyeball—with its sinister rectangular pupil—was tattooed in the center of it. He'd never noticed that detail before and it nearly took his breath away for some reason.

And then his voice got sharp again. Almost like he couldn't help it, he was so frustrated with her. That stupid goat's eye. "When's the last time you spent the night at Dad's house? You just dump that little girl off on the old man and do God knows what all day long."

"Don't you think I know that?"

Dan sighed. "There's nothing I can do for you. You've got to talk to Dad."

"Then get out of my car."

"Fine." Dan barely had time to slam the door before Grace gunned it up the road.

Christ.

5

Afternoon, No Snowfall

The dismissal bell rang, last bell of the school day, shrill and metallic, and Nancy Van Horton watched as the ninth-graders of her Lit-Comp class bolted out of their desks, clumped in the doorway, fighting and tussling, before spilling out into the hallway like horses out the door. Least that's how she saw it. Horses out the door, chasing God knows what.

Her room was empty. Laminated posters covered the white cinder-block walls, posters with famous passages of literature written on them: *Ask not for whom the bell tolls... Whether 'tis nobler in the mind to suffer... And my soul from out that shadow that lies floating on the floor...* Foam-core ceiling, fluorescents buzzing, desktops scratched to hell with graffiti: inverted crosses, *books R 4 faggots,* pentagrams. Standard teenage stuff. Standard high school stuff. Like how they talk and stuff.

Then there was some not-so-standard stuff, stuff she'd remembered through the years, for whatever reason. A specific and very detailed cruciform symbol she'd eventually identified as the Leviathan Cross after she'd looked it up in an occult encyclopedia. Highly detailed, and highly disturbing, tentacled monsters etched into desktops. And one phrase that popped up every couple of years, unaltered, which always made her skin crawl: "We live forever in the mouth of the mouth."

She shuffled through a stack of vocab quizzes on her desk, aimless, graded a few of them, pages bleeding with red ink already, and decided she needed a cigarette. It was a non-smoking building, sure, but no one cared. Nancy got up and went to the door, peeked out, hallways already empty, lockers shut and gleaming. She shut the door, cracked one of the big windows along the wall near her desk and lit a cigarette.

This was one of her quiet moments, those rarest of moments, without all the—

There was a knock at the door.

Cigarette out, tossed out the window, waving her hand, smoke not going anywhere, *shit shit shit.*

"Ms. Van Horton?" A voice on the other side of the door.

Principal Clauson would never address her by her last name. It was someone else, someone who didn't know her, apparently.

"Who is it?" Still waving the smoke around.

"Hapscomb. Detective with the GR police."

Bells went off in Nancy's head. Not unlike school bells. Alarms. *Did he say* detective*?*

She opened the door.

He was tall, not too tall but taller than her, with wide shoulders and a face like a news anchor, square-jawed, dark eyes. He held his suit jacket draped over one shoulder, holding it with his curled index finger—and my God weren't his hands just huge—his other arm resting against the threshold of the door, one shined shoe crossed over the other. Like a catalog model. Nancy never knew real people stood around like that. It was absurd.

"May I come in?" he said.

She turned to the side and motioned for him to enter.

Hapscomb's shoes clacked on the floor as he walked. He passed Nancy, warm wind smelling of aftershave following him. She couldn't help but notice how well-groomed he was. Hair all perfect and brushed, pomaded in place.

"You can pull a chair up to my desk," Nancy said. The aftershave was gone and the cigarette stink was back strong.

The detective draped his jacket over one of the desks in the first row and stood facing the windows, hands palms-down over the clicking radiator that ran the length of the room along the floor. He spoke over his shoulder, "No need for that. I won't be long."

He did not mention the smell of smoke.

Nancy sat behind her desk, started arranging the papers into neat piles, not thinking about it, just doing it.

"Well," she said, slowly, "what can I do for you then?"

"When's the last time you saw Daniel Robertson?"

Totally weird. "This morning. I picked him up along 4 Mile, gave him a ride into town. What's this about? Has Dan done something?"

Hapscomb ignored her questions. "If you were to describe his state of being during your time with him this morning—"

"State of being?"

"Yes, state of being. His disposition, general demeanor."

Nancy paused. She looked at her hands, straightened a ring on her ring finger. She looked up. Hapscomb was still staring out the window. "I guess I'd say that he was upset."

"Upset how? Try to be specific."

"Look, can you tell me what this is about? Or can I see some identification or something?"

Hapscomb turned and held out a black leather bi-fold, flipped it open, revealing an impressive-looking badge, gleaming in the light. GR Police. She'd hadn't seen him take the bi-fold out of his pocket—it was just there—wouldn't have known how to spot a fake, even if it was. Why had she even asked?

She twisted the ring on her finger.

"Dan's mother is sick. He seemed distraught over that."

"What did he say he was doing out by 4 Mile?"

"I don't know. I didn't ask." She thought for a moment. "I figured he was out there with Kenneth Thompkins."

The detective nodded his head, face slack. "And why is that?"

"I saw Kenneth's Jeep there—can't miss the thing. It's spray-painted black with monster truck tires—"

"Kenneth Thompkins is dead."

Nancy heard herself gasp, suddenly aware that the fingers of her left hand had curled into her mouth, pulling at the inside of her bottom lip, tasting stale like tobacco.

She pulled her hand out of her mouth and straightened in her chair. Embarrassed.

"He's what?"

"He's been murdered," Hapscomb said. His eyes were on her eyes. He seemed to be searching for something in her eyes. He did not blink, or if he did, she missed it when he did. She looked away.

"He was a student of mine," she said, "years ago—and not the best one. His kids... His kids are in my class now."

"Heard they haven't been around school lately."

"Yeah." The room seemed smaller somehow. The walls. The walls seemed closer together. Nancy imagined she heard the rush of white noise somewhere outside. Her mouth felt dry.

The posters on the wall. *...It tolls for thee. ...Not to be. ...Nevermore.* She felt anger pulsing through her temples.

"Smoking that meth. Like all the burnouts and dropouts around here. Everyone cooking that shit up in their sheds, in the trailers out by Deadguy Pond. It's a fucking plague." She stared the detective in the eye. "Those kids used to come into this classroom reeking of burnt plastic, eyes as red and glassy as marbles. Like the living dead. That's what they looked like. That's why they haven't been in school. Who knows where they are, what they're doing. And now their dad... I mean, Jesus Christ. Have you heard what Kenneth Jr. carved in his arm?"

6

Early Evening, No Snowfall

The air inside his mother's house was thick with the stench of unwashed flesh. All of the curtains were pulled over the windows. The heating vents rattled, releasing the dusty air of a tired home.

Dan closed the door behind him and took off his Carhartt, hung it on the rack by the door. The skin on his hands was beet-red, itchy.

The house was old—pre-Civil War. All the farmhouses in Ardor were.

Even though Bessie was tucked away behind a closed door, her staleness lingered everywhere. Dan had long ago given up on trying to keep the place presentable, clean. What was the point? Gray piles of dust bunnies clumped together in the corners of every room, the wallpaper sagged—garish streaks of dark yellow paint visible in its folds. What was the point of cleaning it all up if they were just going to sell the place when the old woman died?

After all, he'd been here all his life—in Ardor, in this house. This was the house he'd grown up in, this was the house his asshole father, Harold, had left behind, to repress like so many bad memories. Who needs a family when you're a lotto winner, anyways? Fucking asshole.

Dan pushed open the door to his mother's room and gave himself a second to get used to the smell.

Bessie Robertson had been bed-ridden for almost a month now. Around two weeks ago, her skin had started to release a noxious smell—like baby shit and bad breath. Dan found that it was easiest to get over the smell if he just opened his nostrils wide and took it all in—shocked his system. After that, it was better.

He flicked on the light switch. The pale curtains pulled over the windows seemed to pulse, orange and pink. Outside, the sun was just starting to go down. Dan walked to the side of his mother's bed and sat in a small wooden chair. A clock mounted on the wall audibly ticked away the seconds.

The nightstand was filled with small glass bottles filled with clear liquids, clusters of orange pill canisters, balled-up tissues.

A gray, wool blanket was pulled up to just below Bessie's neckline, arms at her sides, feet exposed, together at the ankles and leaning out to the sides, the shape of a wishbone.

Dan had long been accustomed to the endless nights of constant moaning, the screaming, the crying, the vomiting, the diarrhea. But he'd never been able to accustom himself to her weight-loss. His mother had always been so strong, so healthy.

He reached out and held one of her hands and was reminded of a time when, as a child, he had come across a baby bird lying on the ground in the woods. It had fallen from its nest and lay, crying softly, in a ball. He'd taken the bird in his hands and held it, letting his fingers close with a softness he had never before known was possible.

49

The bird's small belly had pulsed in the palm of his hand as it struggled for breath. The dark brown feathers of its wings were coated in mucus. The bird's eyes were shut. Its small orange beak opened and closed, as if on a timer.

He looked at his mother's face. There was nothing he could've done for that baby bird. And at fifty-six, she still wasn't old. But her face showed the strain of the cancer. Her eyes were sunk in deep, cheeks even deeper. Thick creases radiated from her lips, crawling across her face. Her nose looked unreal, a protrusion of bone.

He squeezed her hand gently and said, "How ya feeling, Ma?"

Bessie wheezed, turned her head on the pillow. Her dark eyelids rolled open. Her eyes were yellow, streaked with thick red veins, pupils gigantic and black.

Her lips parted. "I was dreaming of hallways," she said, voice urgent, surprisingly strong, the strongest it had been in weeks. Her eyes opened a little wider, as if she was emerging from a dream. "I was looking for her in a dark house. Kept bumping into furniture, breaking expensive vases..."

Dan stroked her forearm.

Bessie squeezed her eyes shut. "And there was a door that led to the basement, but the basement was dark and I was so scared...to go into the basement. The furnace was a heart and it was burning. And inside the heart there was the hole."

The doctor had told Dan it was going to be like this. *Stomach cancer is painful, Dan*, he'd said. *It's agonizing.*

50

You're going to have to be strong for her. There's nothing you're going to be able to do except keep her medicated.

They'd taken her to Butterworth Hospital in Grand Rapids. The cancer center went by the name Lettinga, which always sounded to Dan like "Letting go."

None of her surgeries had accomplished much. They'd removed parts of her spleen, her ovaries, her intestine. They were going to set in on the esophagus before Dan decided that enough was enough—that there was no use making what little life she had left even more torturous.

Chemotherapy had been ruled out because the doctor had said it wouldn't be able to undo what the cancer had already done. *Stomach cancer is aggressive. And, unfortunately, not many symptoms show up until it's too late. Your mother's case is advanced. And your health insurance just isn't going to go far enough.*

Dan looked up at the clock on the wall. It would be getting dark soon. He watched the secondhand do a full circle. In ten more minutes he'd be able to give his mother her morphine.

The clock kept ticking.

"It was a horror, Dan," she said. "My dream. Inside the hole there was another hole. And then there was the mouth. The blackness." She struggled over her words.

Dan let go of her hand and turned in his seat. He picked up a bottle, read the label, and put it back down. He picked up another. Another. Couldn't find the morphine. And then, like a weight was dropped, he knew it was gone.

Grace had already been here. She'd taken it. Jesus.

51

She seemed to read his face. "She was here, Dan. I told her it was okay. She needs it more than I do."

He ignored her, furious, found the Hydrocodone. Christ, only reason Grace didn't steal these things is because they were too weak for her. He'd have to feed her pills by hand. "Just close your eyes, Ma. We're gonna give you your pills."

Dan plucked one of the white, bar-shaped pills from the canister and held it between two fingers. A series of numbers and letters was etched on its flat belly.

Dan pressed down on the tip of Bessie's chin with the thumb of his left hand, opening her mouth. The tips of her teeth poked out from behind her lips. He thought of Kenneth.

He placed the pill on Bessie's tongue, picked up a glass of water from the nightstand, poured a small amount into her mouth, then turned his hand and placed the tips of his fingers on the underside of her chin. He pushed her mouth shut and felt the tight knot of the salivary gland tucked away beneath her jawbone, like a golf ball.

He massaged her neck with the palm of his hand, stroked up and down, up and down. A lump passed through Bessie's throat. The pill had gone down. Two more to go.

The clock kept ticking.

When he was done, she stared at him, unblinking. "I was in the mouth of the mouth," she said. And repeated it. And repeated it. And then fell into something fitful, only slightly resembling sleep.

He shut the door behind him, and with all the speed and energy of a man who had done a day's worth of hard labor, Dan Robertson crept down the hall to his bedroom. The house was dark now—the winter sun disappeared behind its black veil.

Without undressing, Dan fell into his bed. He fell asleep almost instantly.

He was in a clearing in the woods. The boat launch. All around him, the jingling of a bicycle bell. The rushing water sounding like a baseball card flapping against the spokes of a wheel.

The sky was sleek and silver.

The branches of the blackened tree rose up into the sky, spread forth like a web of veins. There, over there, was the blue tarp staked to the ground.

Dan walked toward the tarp, his footing unsure over the lumpy ground, soft with moving shapes, as if buried bodies struggled beneath his footsteps.

The roar of the river began to fade—getting softer, quieting down—and then it was gone. The silence was thick and heavy—the quiet of a storm, the negative suck of a vacuum.

He came to a stop, standing before the tarp, lumpy ground still shifting beneath him.

There was a loud snapping noise, and then another. One side of the tarp lifted off the ground, as if Kenneth was pushing upward. Another snapping noise. The five-inch metal stakes raising up, out of the ground.

The tarp fell forward.

The roar of the river flooded the silence, shedding the sound of jingling bells. Kenneth sat before him, his back straight. Snow obscured his face—cracked and dry like makeup, his eyes blacked by shadow. The red of his flannel like a pool of blood beneath the ice.

"I'm dead," Kenneth said. His voice was clear and distinct, resounding everywhere.

Dan felt himself freezing, heard the ice cracking as it solidified on his cheeks, spreading out from his armpits, down the inside of his biceps.

"I'm dead," Kenneth repeated. "Your mother is dead."

"That's not true," Dan said. He tried to take a step forward. The soles of his Timberlands had frozen to the ground. He ripped his right foot free. His foot came down with a crunch and froze in place.

The ice spread farther down Dan's arms, out from under the sleeves of his jacket. With stiff movements, Dan held his hand up before his face. He watched as the ice webbed brilliant crystal patterns across his palm.

"I'm dead," Kenneth said. "Your mother is dead."

Dan opened his mouth—he wanted to scream, to yell—but no sound would come. The water was everywhere, all around him like a total blackness, filling the clearing, pushing out against the naked trees that stood straight like bones planted in the ground. The ice crept into Dan's mouth. And then shards of ice and streams of dirt poured out of his mouth and hit the ground. It sounded like the river.

~

The sound of breaking glass woke Dan from his sleep. His heart was pounding. His window was open, curtains blowing. The room was freezing.

Someone's in the house. He leapt out of bed, cracked his bedroom door.

Loud thumps and the sound of a muffled voice echoed up the stairway. Whatever was left of the dream vanished completely.

Shit, this is really happening.

7

Late Evening, No Snowfall

Grace Robertson always dated bad boys. She was attracted to flash.

By the time she was a freshman in high school she'd already gotten high with a couple of seniors, football players, Scud Reilly and Gooch Jailer, had let both of them feel her up at the same time, back in the woods behind the portables of the junior high, and she hadn't minded, not at all.

She'd had a body like a woman by the time she was thirteen—all the things guys noticed: big lips, hips, tits that even a sweatshirt couldn't hide.

She went for the guys with the varsity letters—at first. But they turned out to be boring, blockheads. So she went for the shop guys, the guys with the hot cars, Chevy pickups, old Vettes, Mustangs, she loved Mustangs. She smoked dope, sometimes theirs, sometimes her own, didn't matter how dirty it was, or expensive—just as long as they didn't try to brag about it, she hated it when they bragged about it.

Every day, during her lunch hour, she'd tool around with a different guy, get high, make out a little, watch them shift gears with their big blue-veined hands. It turned her on. It made her want to fuck. If they promised to buy her a bottle of Goldschlager then she'd party with them.

She first gave it up to Charlie McGrath, a loser, a rosy-cheeked wild-child rich kid who had his own GTO, fully paid for. He'd been rough with her, tore the buttons on her shirt, ripped the hooks on her bra after fumbling with it for a minute or two. He'd pinned her in the back of his car, early on a winter morning before school, and it had been so cold that their breath had been visible, great clouds of it, shooting back and forth with their breathing. They kept their clothes on, just unzipped their flies. She told Ashley Banks later that day that she couldn't imagine a worse way to lose it. "Hell," she said, "his thumbs felt like ice when he reached up my shirt and squeezed my tits. Even his dick felt cold." But he'd had good weed and she was tired of saying no.

She developed a reputation. The girl who would huff spray-paint out of a tube sock, stumble out of back rooms at house parties, her red lips ringed with sparkly silver paint. The girl who'd give head if you gave her a ride home from school. The girl who fucked. Who let boys put it in her ass. Who let biker dudes tattoo crazy shit on her back with homemade pens. The girl who knew older guys, guys that could get shit from the blacks in Detroit: coke, guns, crates of cigarettes. The girl who knew about all the lakefront parties, parties with the prissy rich kids from the east side of Grand Rapids, parties with guys from the Amway plant, parties that no one else ever heard about, where weird shit would go down in back rooms.

She was always looking for more, always wanting more. Her appetite was legendary. Because Grace

Robertson was one of the bad girls. And that's how she liked it.

"Sweet Baby Clayton got himself blowed up real bad—we heard he were jus' a skinless shriveled mess." Lawrence Newbert spit out a tan stream of Skoal, swept the stringy hair out of his eyes and adjusted his mesh-back baseball cap. A massive black flag with the white lightning-bolt SS symbols hung on the wall behind him. "Little baby boy was out cookin' in the woods, using one of Fox's old sheds."

Grace lit a cigarette, sucked on it hard. She'd heard plenty of horror stories like this one, plenty of scare stories about people turning into fireballs, about trailers torn wide open, as if the meth churned up a tiny tornado, a flash-fire rage, and twisted everything around it like it was just a nothing. But those stories had never been about anyone she'd actually known.

The Newbert brothers: Lawrence, Teddy, and Sweet Baby Clayton.

But now there were only two.

They lived up at the winding end of Ardor's most notorious backwater shithole: Bolt Street. True woodsmen: never went to school, never paid taxes, learned to shoot guns and drive trucks and skin animals all before they'd so much as mastered a toothbrush. They were rumored to have abducted, tortured, and killed a census worker some years back. The land around their trailer was cluttered with rusted-out cars, scrapped school buses, refrigerators stripped of their motors, their doors, bullet-hole riddled road signs, you name it, so crowded with metal and rust that the county had to declare it a salvage yard, not that anyone would be dumb enough to go up Bolt Street and pick through nothing belonging to the brothers.

"Sweet Baby Clayton always did have a death wish," Teddy said, his eyes dropping to the floor. "Hadn't slept for nearly a week when he went out there. Clawing at the skin on his arm talking about bugs in his bloodstream, bugs with human heads. It was spooky. Bound to make mistakes when you been awake that long, you ask me."

Lawrence came back to the table—a foldout, plastic thing covered in green felt—and set down three Coors tallboys. "Man, I tell you," he sat down and cracked open one of the beers, foam bubbling up over his knuckles, "we can't cook enough to meet demand. We make a batch, haul it into town, barely got time to count our money before the phone's going crazy again. Little brother was loving the life."

"Listen," Grace said, stubbing out her cigarette. "That's what I need to talk to you guys about—supply and demand. Business. There's going to be more money down the road. We all know that. But right now I can't pay you. I'm waiting for my guy in Detroit to make things right, but he got hog-tied and left to die right there in his living room. Niggers stole everything from him, even his shoes. So I'm gonna need an advance."

Lawrence blew up with laughter so hard Grace nearly pissed herself. He slapped his thigh and stomped the ground with one of his steel-toed boots. He looked at Grace and smiled, tobacco juice dribbling down his black beard.

He leaned forward in his seat, rolled up the sleeves of the long-underwear he wore beneath his blue flannel. Crude, overlapping, blue-ink prison tattoos covered his arms. Topless nuns and pin-ups and M-16s. Straight razors and swastikas. He even had a tattoo of Babs Bunny bending over and sticking a carrot up her pussy. Each finger on his hand was tattooed with a crooked inverted cross near the top, pointed tridents below those, each knuckle lettered to spell out S-C-U-M F-U-C-K. His elbows were both webbed. He claimed that half his tattoos were done with the ash from torched garbage and goat urine. "We jus' explained to you that our baby brother's body looks like a California raisin and all you got to say is you need an advance?" He shook his head, still laughing. "My God, Gracie. You ain't got no heart at all, do you?"

Grace smiled, sipped her beer, gave Lawrence the finger. "Fuck you."

"You're being serious, ain't you?"

"As all hell."

"Well shit," Teddy said. "Looks like Lawrence and me are just gonna have to fuck you then."

The room was tense. Nothing but the sound of... Of what? Of like the little bubbles hissing inside her beer can. Could she really hear that?

"On account of you not having the money you owe us, you know, for the drugs we gave you free of charge," Lawrence said, standing, the clack of his belt buckle, the zip of his fly, and then his jeans were around his ankles and he was already hard. "Fair's fair, little girl." He lifted his work shirt over his head, revealing a torso-sized goat skull.

Its eye sockets ringed each nipple, horns curling up and around his shoulders. Across his lower stomach, in thuggish, Gothic lettering, the phrase "Hail Bornless."

And Grace was on her knees, making her way around the table to him.

Teddy crossed the room and slapped some old record onto the turntable—the crackle and hiss, speakers swelling with fuzz. And when it started, when the music came on, Grace recognized it as something familiar from stoner parties back in high school, recognized it as the first Saint Vitus record. And the first sludgy guitar riffs were wobbling out those cheap speakers as Grace took Lawrence's cock into her mouth, just a sour, skinny little thing, her forehead coming up against his soft belly. She felt Teddy come up behind her and palm the back of her skull, pushing down, down, making her swallow more and more of his brother's disgusting dick, beyond choking until she felt a feeling like nothing at all, like she was herself but like, years ago, listening to Saint Vitus for the first time and feeling so sexy and so cool that she didn't hardly know what to do about it.

There's a giant worm that lives in the concrete tunnels beneath the big sewer grate by the water treatment facility. I know this for a fact. It's fifty feet long, a hundred feet long, and it's as old as time itself. Bicycle Bob told me that it eats kids and homeless people that wander down there, that it like stores them in its stomach, and keeps them alive forever.

It doesn't have a name. It's just The Worm—pink like a baby rat, the color of flesh. One end tapers off into a point and that's its tail, and the other end is just a big, gaping mouth lined with six or seven rows of triangular teeth, like shark teeth but only sharper and probably bigger, too.

One of these days, when the world's gonna end, Bicycle Bob said, the Worm is supposed to curl up in a ring and start eating its own tail, and when it does that, when it eats itself, it'll travel beyond time, taking all them people living in its stomach with it, where they can live forever somewhere even farther away than as much of outer space as you can possibly imagine. We live forever in the mouth of the mouth, he said.

I know this sounds stupid, but it's the truth—I know it for a fact.

I started dreaming about The Worm when I was six or seven or so—after all that terrible stuff happened. At Silver Creek. After Bicycle Bob put the worm in me.

I'd be in the woods by the creek, you know, the one that goes all the way to the big sewer grate with the big iron bars. And everything is real clear, like on a summer day. Everything is real vibrant. Like the trees look extra brown, the trees look real green.

And then I see this little girl that looks like me, she's real far away, though, like through the trees, like when you see the shining of a river through the trees, wearing a jean jacket with her hair hanging down to the center of her back, and she's walking through that big grate entrance, turning sideways and slipping between two of those big bars. She's slipping through those iron bars and into the darkness and I want to yell something to her, like Stop, don't go in there. But I don't got no voice, no sound comes out of my mouth.

And I can't go nowhere, can't go in that sewer 'cause the dark is just too creepy. But I hear the sound of a child's laughter echoing down from above me. It's me. The laughter. I'm laughing 'cause I know The Worm will never take me, not the way I am. I look up but there's only darkness above me. It needs someone pure. And I'm not pure. It needs a virgin.

And that laughter just keeps echoing all around me.

1

Earlier that Morning, Heavy Snowfall

Back in the '50s, a couple of Ardor's most enterprising citizens came together and converted the basement of St. Mary's, an old gray-stone church at the edge of town, into a fully functioning bar. There was no floor, just dirt, the ceiling just blood-and-guts plumbing. No one bothered with a liquor license or whatever. They just tacked some plywood together, hung a dartboard on the wall, brought in thirty bottles of booze, a couple of kegs, and opened up shop. Named the place "Rose's" on account of the lady who served the drinks. Church service was still held every Sunday—for the dozen or so people who showed up—and the bar opened immediately afterward, stayed open until next Sunday morning.

Tom Lucas and Sammy and Bill were sitting in a row, elbows up on the bar, Willie Nelson's "Stardust" playing from a cheap stereo, feeling sad, sludging up everyone's drunk, making things all introspective. The momentum of the daylong drinking binge was starting to waver.

Tom took down his fourteenth double of Wild Turkey, puffed out his red cheeks like a trumpet player and blew. His forehead was beaded with sweat. "God I'm drunk," he said. He turned round on his stool, leaned back against the bar. The room split up the middle at an angle, separated, pulled away from itself, but snapped back together, pulled away, snapped back together. He rubbed his eyes with his thumb and index finger. "Jesus, I feel like shit."

Sammy slowly leaned forward, nestled his head in his folded arms. He grunted once or twice in response. He snored a bit, out cold again.

Bill was still going strong, having stuck to beer since his first double. But they'd been drinking for so many hours, since what? Two or three in the afternoon? They'd been getting round after round after round so quickly, that he was swollen with liquid, getting mouthy, brash. Bill was one of those guys who never quit drinking once he started, either fell asleep or got punched out, but he never quit. Sometimes he'd black out just standing there, still talking to you, but like with nothing behind his eyes, just jabbering on about whatever. And then in the morning, hung over to shit, he'd always be the first one to come round calling, asking if he'd said anything stupid or glassed someone or groped anyone's girlfriend or something like that.

Rose, a squat old lady with a wrinkled mouth, had her arms crossed under her huge heavy tits. She was the blood of this place and everyone knew it—the kind of local who'd never traveled beyond state lines, who'd somehow found a way to eke out a living. "You boys 'bout had enough, now?" Her eyes were squinted small, slathered in bright blue shadow. She'd seen this sort of drinking before—saw it quite often, really—and knew that it never led nowhere good.

"Tell us more about the detective," Bill said, grabbing up a couple of darts off the bar.

Tom swung his heavy head, all slow, like a dinosaur. "Yeah, Tupper. The 'tective."

At the end of the bar, head lolling on his shoulders, sat Derrick Tupper—still in his uniform—a mug half-filled with foam in front of him, couple empty shot glasses and a crushed-up soft-pack of Reds. He'd been going at it that night just as hard as any of the regular boys, taking hits of crank out in his car when he felt himself tiring out. He blinked a bit at Tom, burped.

"He called you a dumb fucker," Derrick said, pointing at Tom. And then laughed. "But don't worry, I'll set him straight."

"And how you gonna do that?" Tom said. "Barely even old enough to hold that gun a'yours. What makes you think he's gonna lissen to a fuckwad like you?"

"I told you earlier, there's nothing to worry about. He just wants to talk to you, that's all. Ask you some questions."

"This shit's gotten out of control," Sammy mumbled, muffled, his head still in his arms.

"You shut up," Tom said.

Derrick nodded. "I told you guys. It's no big deal. Everything's just protocol."

"The thing I don't get," Tom said, "is how the fuck all this happened."

"Tom," Derrick said, "listen, this dick thinks Robertson's the one whose story don't make any sense. I even mentioned to him that Robertson is a weirdo. Said his story had too many holes. Too many questions."

Rose stepped forward. "You boys talking about Daniel?"

"What's it matter to you?" Bill said.

"I wasn't listening to you," she said. "So shut your goddamned mouths before the flies make a home. And even if I was listening to you, don't think for a second I'd ever go talking to no shithead cop. I don't say boo. Stupid shits." She glared at Derrick. Stuck out her chin, and shuffled off to the other end of the bar.

"Jesus God," Tom said.

"Listen to me, Tom, just listen for a sec," Derrick said. "It's like I said. There ain't nothing for you all to worry about. Robertson's clearly making up stories and the dick, he's a smart guy. He sees right through that creep's bullshit. I mean, whatever happened out there today—"

"Still ain't none of your business," Tom said.

Derrick kept his mouth shut, nodded again. He knew better than to talk back to someone like Tom Lucas. It's not like they were at the station or something. This was Tom's game, his arena, his word was law. Plus, Tom was Derrick's only hookup for meth now that Fox got sent up and he'd burned his bridge with Grace.

"'Cept, the only thing is, you're gonna have to talk to this dick eventually, either that or he'll drag you in. Or make me do it."

"And why's that?" Tom said.

"Well now that the thing's been ruled a homicide—"

"Whoa, now," Bill cut in. "No one never said nothing about no homicide."

"It's no big deal. It's like I told you. There's a protocol to this sort of thing. It's all protocol. You just have to come in," he checked his watch, eyes went wide, "Jesus, it's the morning. So just come in sometime later this morning, stick to your story and then you'll get to leave."

"Mother fuck this shit," Tom said, sliding off his bar stool, knocking it to the floor. The crash shook the sleepy, slow room. Sammy shot up straight with a gasp, looking around all wild.

"That's it," Rose said. "Bar's closed."

Tom pointed a finger at Derrick. "If anything goes wrong, it's your fucking fault, Tupper."

"But what the hell did I—"

"Your fucking fault," Tom repeated. His face was coated in a sheen of sweat, both eyelids at half-mast, mouth hanging open. "But don't think for a second that I ain't gonna protect myself."

And the big man was gone, stumbled his way outside, everyone else too drunk or too lazy or too frightened to do anything about it.

"Jesus," Derrick said.

"Sometimes it's best to not tell Tom nothing that'll make him angry," Bill said. "One last round of doubles and beers, Rose."

Sammy lifted his head, mumbled "Let's all stay here forever." His eyes were still shut.

The old lady frowned.

Bill shrugged, closed one eye, held up a dart, pumped his arm a few times, and tossed it at the board. It went wide and bounced off the stone wall.

2

Just Before Dawn, Heavy Snowfall

White-knuckled, Dan clasped the handrail as he slowly descended the staircase. It was dark. His entire body was stiff with fear.

He reached the bottom of the stairs, stood still, listened. Whoever was breaking in was having a hard time of it. There was a lot of grunting, a lot of heaving, heavy breathing, noises like someone was kicking at the aluminum siding on the outside of the house—sharp, clacking noises, slightly muffled through the thin walls.

Dan's hand found his heart, almost instinctively. It was beating so hard it hurt.

The house went quiet. The wind howled outside. The house moaned. Dan held his breath. The sounds of his beating heart filled his ears. He counted his heartbeats, counted up to six before the grunting and the heaving started again. And louder this time.

The fucker's stuck in the window. Dan rushed through the blackness of the dining room, stood in the doorway leading into the living room, kept the right half of his body behind the doorframe, curled his left hand around the eave, pinched the light switch between two fingers, took a deep breath and flipped it on.

The living room filled with a buzzing, yellow light.

Tom Lucas. His body was slung over the window sill, stomach down—his top half inside, bottom half outside.

His Carhartt was streaked with dried mud, meaty knuckles resting hanging low, cut to shit, shedding globs of black blood onto the floorboards. Bits of broken glass—jagged pieces of varying size—littered the floor around the window. Snowflakes the size of dimes twirled their way through the open window, sticking in Tom's hair, melting into quivering drops of water.

Tom's head was turned to the side, hanging slack, his cheek was pressed against the thin strip of wall beneath the window. The black skullcap he'd been wearing earlier in the day was gone.

The sour stink of bourbon filled the room. The bastard was drunk, asleep, stuck in the window.

And then Tom's eyes rolled open. He turned his head so his chin was resting on the wall. His eyes were bright red, glassy, distant, like there was nothing but clouds of smoke behind them, a head full of a whole lot of nothing.

The bastard dragged his listless hands up off the floor, placed them palms-down on the sill, at his sides. His elbows bent and he pushed up, straightening out his arms, feet kicking and scraping at the aluminum siding, like he was trying to climb but couldn't find footing. His face was purpling. And then his head dipped forward, a rush of movement, swinging at an arc toward the floor; his torso followed, poured through the window like fluid.

Tom crashed to the floor, landed hard on his shoulder, bits of glass crunching beneath his weight.

Dan didn't know whether to call the cops or laugh. "Tom?" He didn't know what to say. "Tom, what the hell are you doing?"

Tom grunted. And then he was snoring again, face down on the floor, head turned to the side. His eyes were shut. His eyelids fluttered like he was dreaming.

The wind kept howling. Snow blew in through the open window, started collecting in sloping piles in the corner. The house groaned as the furnace kicked on in the basement.

Tom's snore ground like crunching gears and his eyes opened. He pushed up off the floor, flopped onto his side. He looked around the room. His eyes locked onto Dan.

"Robertson, you fucker." He slurred his speech, barely moved his mouth as he spoke. "Don't do as you're told. Lousy fucker."

Dan had backed up against the wall.

Tom was on his knees, coughing, the smell of whiskey everywhere like a stinging sharp cloud.

And before Dan could even react, Tom was up on his feet, wavering. He took a step back, a step forward, then to the side.

He nearly tripped over the couch, laughing like a kid on his first drunk. A truly joyful laugh.

"Lousy fucker."

Tom leaned into a stride, legs jerking, went diagonal across the room a few steps, shifted his weight, lost his balance, backed up into the dead and brown and brittle Christmas tree in the corner. Had they really left that thing out since Christmas? Jesus. He rocked on his heels and fell into it, dropping down hard onto his ass. The tree showered dry needles.

The smell of pine cut into the whiskey stench. Dan thought of his mother upstairs, didn't want her to wake to this, didn't want her to be frightened.

Tom sat on the ground with his legs stretched out before him, toes pointing toward the ceiling. His chin rested on his chest, head nodding with each breath.

The light on the ceiling buzzed. The cold rattle of Tom's idling pickup truck outside.

Hapscomb's number was in Dan's wallet, upstairs on the nightstand next to his bed. He could just go and get it, pick up the phone and—

"Ya dumb fuck, ya," Tom said. "Think you know alls that's going on? Fucker. Bitches stole my gun and you— dumb-fuck—asking me where's it gone?"

Tom's gun? But he said it was Kenneth's...

"Bunch of lousy bitches think they can take what belongs to me?" Tom thumped a fist against his chest, leaving a dark smudge of blood on his jacket. "I'm fucking Tom fucking Lucas, God dammit. I'll fucking kill ever-one who takes shit from me and tries to fuck me."

Tom's face hung slack. The corners of his mouth pulled down in a bulldog frown. "I don't know how they got it, but they did. What belonged to me and they just took it. I'll kill those lousy murdering fucks as soon as I find 'em."

Dan's heart pounded in his throat. His mouth tasted like shit. "Who, Tom? Who's a murdering fuck?"

Tom's head dropped back as he raised his chin up in the air. "You're a fuck, Robbers." He laughed the childish laugh again.

A burp bubbled up and seeped out Tom's open mouth. The smell of bile and burp and whiskey and pine. Enough to make you sick.

"There's plenny ah shit that goes on in Ardor than crosses paths with the creepy cemetery keeper," Tom said. "You just get it all at the end...don't see it as it's going on around you. In the woods... Know what I mean? There's scary shit'll make your blood run cold, Robbers. You got no direct connection to nothing. Just stack up dead folks in piles. Fucking creeps work a job like that. And you're the biggest creep of 'em all—always have been." He took a deep breath. "Everyone thinks you have sex with dead bodies." And then he was laughing like crazy again. "Dead-body fucker."

He lifted his arm up and held it out straight before him, put two fingers together and pointed them at Dan like a gun, shut one eye like he was taking aim, the tip of his tongue jutting out the corner of his mouth. "Pow." He dropped his hand into his lap, kept on laughing.

"Robbers," Tom said, "I came here tonight to fuck you up." He exhaled, paused. "And I plan on doing just that." His head seemed too heavy for his neck, bobbling on his shoulders like a jack-in-the-box.

Dan was still backed against the wall. "It's about time you get up on out of here. Before either of us does something stupid, something we'll regret."

That big gap-toothed smile. Tom's head rested on his shoulder, one eye shut, the other one rolled back in its socket.

"No, let's both do something we'll regret, yeah, Robbers? 'Cause like I said, I came here to fuck you up and I'm not leaving until I do what I came here to do."

Tom groaned as he leaned forward and took a knee. "Lord," he said.

And then he was up—up on two feet—shambling like a zombie in a horror film. His red eyes. Dan turned and lunged for the door, heard Tom's boot stomps behind him, felt Tom's massive hand close up on the back of his neck. He spun Dan around and threw him back against the wall. Tom fumbled his hands around Dan's voice box, trying to get a grip.

Face flushed with blood-rush, the toes of his work boots scrambling against the floor, edges of his vision bleeding black shapes, blobs of negative light. Tom opened his mouth and screamed in Dan's face, showing the silver fillings in his molars. Struggling, the two men lost their balance. The black ooze swallowed up all of the light and the whipping, white noise of wind filled Dan's ears as he came down hard on his hip and felt his head smack the floor.

Dan opened his eyes, saw two versions of his living room ceiling—the dull, orange star of light buzzing directly above him. The two ceilings pulled together and merged into one.

He rubbed his shoulder and was surprised to not find fishing line stitched into his skin.

Alone. He was alone. A trail of wet boot tracks led from the living room, into the dining room, and probably right on out through the front door, too.

The pile of snow beneath the window had grown deep, maybe an inch, inch and a half. The stink of Tom's bourbon still lingered.

Dan stumbled over to the couch, sank into its ancient cushions.

He sat there for nearly half an hour, shivering from the cold, crying but not really crying. Grasping at thoughts.

When he felt himself calming down, Dan went into the kitchen, opened the pantry beneath the sink, and got out a garbage bag, a roll of duct tape, and a pair of scissors. He cut the bag open along its fold and taped it over the broken window. The wind outside sucked and pulled on the bag.

His mother would be waking up soon. She would need to be changed and fed. Dan bided his time, waiting to hear her moans through the ceiling.

3

Sunrise, Light Snowfall

Hapscomb rolled over in bed, fumbled for the walkie-talkie on the nightstand, hissing scrambled static, the white smarting sun filling his single room at the Motel 6, a cleansing light that brought forth the worst of the room's furnishings, the drabness of the cheap desk and TV cabinet, the dullness of the gray carpet.

Too tired to even check the time. Room freezing cold. Hapscomb held down the talk button. "What's it?"

"Better come down to CRD 154." Hal Miller. "Near the covered bridge. I'll have someone radio you directions once you get to your car. When you get close you'll see the lights."

"Slow down a second, what's happened?"

"There's been an accident."

"I said tell me what happened."

"It's Tom Lucas. He's dead."

The covered bridge was a town landmark, refurbished every five or ten years. It was a remarkable piece of carpentry, solid, sturdy, painted brown, an easily identifiable image of old-time country living, something that graced the covers of the touristy pamphlets in the little gift shop on Main.

Hapscomb got out of his car just before the opening of the bridge. Miller was right. He'd been able to see the red and blue lights from nearly a hundred yards down the road. Two squads, an ambulance and, no joke, a fire truck. In small towns everyone answered the same call.

The waters of the Thornapple churned, an icy grinding noise; this bridge was only about two hundred yards upstream from where they'd found Thompkins' body the day before.

The front end of Tom Lucas's Ram was wrapped snug around the rock-solid body of an aged oak. All of the windows in the cab were blown out, the big dumb oaf slung over the wheel, airbag a big deflated balloon, powder everywhere, his head looking scorched with dried blood, one hand hanging out the window.

"Glad I finally got to meet you, Mr. Lucas," Hapscomb said. And then felt stupid for it. Because it wasn't funny and there was no one around to hear it. So much for an attempt at humor.

Hal waved to him as he made his way up the snowy road. The flakes were falling, though they were small, not sticking, tossed around in the light winds like so much dust. "You don't fuck around, do you, Hapscomb? Made it here in record time."

Hapscomb took Hal's outstretched hand and gave it a solid pump. So official. He was always so official. It made him want to scream sometimes. "Seemed pretty important." He took a few steps closer to the truck, tried to get a better look inside.

"He was dead when we got here," Hal said. "Looks like we've got another one for the morgue in Forest Hills."

"Jesus, you can smell the whiskey from here," Hapscomb said. He pinched shut his nostrils as he leaned closer, again angling to get a better look at Lucas.

"Can smell the shit, too," Hal said, turning, making his way over to the uniforms by the squads. Hapscomb heard him bark at the ambulance driver and an EMT to remove the body and load it up.

Something wasn't quite right, something with Lucas's hands. They were all shredded up, gouged up like he'd been punching out windows, the cuts all grisly and bloodied. He bent his knees, leaned to the side, tried to get a look at Lucas's face. The eyes were shut. Nose was pulped, the cartilage destroyed, just a hanging shred of skin. Great gobs of blood had frozen around the nostrils, the open mouth, front teeth shattered and both lips split up the middle. Hapscomb looked down Tom's throat. It was packed with dried blood, a black plug. Like he'd choked on it. Jesus.

He stood up straight and called out to Hal. "Any idea where Lucas was last night?"

"Not yet."

Hapscomb thought for a moment. "Which way is Dan Robertson's house from here?"

Hal pointed over Hapscomb's shoulder. "Straight back thataway."

Hapscomb looked over his shoulder. In all his years as a beat cop, all his time as a detective, he'd learned to trust a hunch when he felt one.

4

Morning, Light Snowfall

After the third or fourth blast of a car horn, Dan finally pulled back the curtain in his mother's bedroom window, steeled his nerves to peek out over the window ledge and see who was out there.

He was surprised to see Hapscomb, standing beside his car in the ice-cracked driveway, leaning against the door, one hand in his pocket, the other through the rolled-down window, blasting the horn. He looked straight up at Dan, eyes hidden behind dark glasses, the black shades gleaming with white light. Not smiling. Jesus, who did he think it would be? Dan let the curtain fall back into place, took a step back from the window. Why hadn't Hapscomb called? Were the phones still out? He hadn't even checked. Either way, he'd been seen. There was nowhere to go now, nowhere to go except outside and nothing to do except talk to the detective. And when he walked out the front door, taking care to button up his Carhartt around a scarf so it covered the finger-sized bruises on his extremely tender neck, Dan was more than relieved to see that enough snow had fallen since early morning to erase any tracks Tom's truck might've left behind. Everything was pristine. Nothing had happened. And he silently prayed to himself that he could just stay uninvolved for as long as this thing went on, that he wouldn't have to answer any more questions, say anything else about anything, that he could just be left to do what he was best at: tend to the cemetery, tend to his mother. Alone.

But it was too late for that already, wasn't it?

"We're going for a ride, Robertson," Hapscomb said as Dan approached. He cracked open his door, gestured with his head and said, "Come on, get in."

Dan hesitated. "Where are we going?"

Hapscomb took off his glasses. His eyes were cold and blue, haloed by the sun-shined snow. "Haven't you heard yet?"

Dan shook his head.

"Tom Lucas is dead."

The words didn't register, not really, and Dan showed no sign of surprise, of shock or worry or whatever. It could've been a lie, some police tactic or something, for all he knew. "So what do you want me to do about it?" Dan was surprised at his own words, at the force with which he delivered them.

Hapscomb cocked his head to the side, looked like he was about to laugh or something but he didn't, and his chin sort of like sunk into his neck like he'd tasted something terrible. "I don't expect you to do anything about it. Except make a positive ID."

"Can't you get anyone in town to do that? I've got to stay here and look after my mom. She's not well, you know."

"I don't want just *anyone*—I want *you*. Plus, I think we got some things to talk about."

Dan was about to argue when Hapscomb cut him off, waved his hand like *I don't want to hear it.*

80

"Your mom's gonna be fine. The hospice workers come during the day, don't they? Ten to three? And they have a key, right? That's what they told me when I spoke with them. She'll be fine. We both know that. Also, I'm not asking and never have been, so get in the car."

There was nothing Dan could do. He was trapped. He'd have to get in the car.

That familiar gray blur of the trees whipping by the sides of the road. They rode in silence for a few minutes, sliding along the back roads, turned onto the Beltline and picked up speed. Hapscomb cleared his throat.

"So there's one question I've been dying to ask you since I met you yesterday," Hapscomb said.

They were gliding along, walls of massive evergreens at their sides, rolling hills into the horizon, putting miles behind them, between them and Ardor. At the rate Hapscomb was driving, Dan figured they'd be in Forest Hills in less than fifteen minutes. Every once in a while an Amway truck would barrel by, spraying their windshield with slushy ice. The sky was a silent and cracked gray. Beautiful overcast.

"What's that?"

"How do you bury dead bodies in the ground if the ground is frozen? At the cemetery, I mean."

"Got a little Bobcat, an excavator. Town voted and paid for it decades ago. Gets traded in every few years. Thing's not so hard to use."

"And you do all that work by yourself?"

"Hire out to some high schoolers looking for extra money in the summer, pay 'em in cash, when we do the grounds keeping and fix any damage incurred during the winter. Fallen trees branches, broken fencing, tipped-over gravestones."

Hapscomb gave Dan an inquisitive look. "Oh yeah?"

"You'd be surprised. All sorts of desecration goes on. There's one mausoleum we got there, belongs to the family of the town's founders. Seems like every year that thing gets broken into. They paint pentagrams in there, on the walls. Leave their underwear on the ground, used condoms. It's kids, I think. Has to be. Little devil-worshippers." Dan felt himself relaxing, easing into the conversation. It was okay for him, easy for him to talk about the things he knew, when his brain didn't have to scramble for answers, figure out what was the best thing to say, the least weird or questionable thing.

"My family had goats when I was a kid," Dan continued. "We used to keep them fenced up behind the house. Didn't matter how high the fence was, those little goats would still find a way to scramble up and over it. So we'd tear it down, build it up again, maybe a foot or two taller this time. Within a week they'd be getting over that, too."

Hapscomb stayed silent, let Dan talk, knew enough to know that this was a good sign.

"That's sort of the way it is with the cemetery. Doesn't matter if we lock the gates, or if we put barbed wire over the walls. The kids will always find a way to get in. It's like they're drawn to the place, like they get a rush from it. Even used to happen when I was their age." Dan's voice faded, went soft a bit, like he was remembering something painful, a time in his life he'd rather forget. "Kids were always going to the graveyard to have sex, do drugs, drink beer. But now... Things feel like they've gotten worse somehow. The things they write on the walls, they're getting weirder."

"Like what?" Hapscomb said. "What do they write?"

Dan sat there for a few seconds, thinking. And then, "Anyone told you about Bicycle Bob yet?"

Hapscomb shook his head. "No." He waited.

"He was someone who lived out in the woods," Dan said, speaking slowly, as if he was choosing his words extra carefully. "That's what everyone thinks, at least. He used to take kids. I saw him once. With Bill Peterson. Other people in town said they've seen him, too. But they didn't describe him like the way I remembered. Even Bill saw him different."

"He took kids?" Hapscomb asked.

"Yes. Abducted them. Tortured them. That's what the stories said. And..." Dan stopped himself. There was no reason to tell the detective about Grace. He'd gotten carried away in the first place to even say this much. Gotten too comfortable.

"And what?"

"Nothing," Dan said. "Just kid's stories."

"Why do they call him that? Bicycle Bob?"

"They say, when he was a kid, he used to ride one of those three-wheeled bikes with the big basket in the back. You know the kind? Apparently he'd have that whole basket stuffed with naked, porcelain dolls. Antiques. With the glass eyes. They say he used to ride that bike around downtown, taking up the whole sidewalk, jingling his bell when he came up behind people, scaring the shit out of 'em."

"You know, I called your house round ten last night. Once the phones were fixed."

"Oh? Did you?" Dan was thankful for the abrupt change in subject.

"No one picked up."

"I musta been sleeping."

Hapscomb turned in his seat. Dan couldn't read anything in the face hidden behind those dark glasses. "You got someone who can corroborate that?" But then he cracked a smile, and just like that he was looking back out the windshield, focusing on his driving again, and Dan could barely catch his breath because he'd been disarmed so quickly, so effortlessly—all his comfort had melted away and left him almost literally gasping for a response. Jesus Christ, this guy was always working.

"I make you uneasy, don't I?"

Always working and he was good at his job, too. Dan didn't see any point in lying. "You do."

"Why?"

Dan looked at Hapscomb. He'd opened up the honesty floodgates, no point in stopping now. It was hopeless either way. "Because I'm mixed up in something bigger than me, I know that. And I'm scared."

Hapscomb laughed, actually chuckled.

"That's funny?"

"No, it's not funny. I'm sorry. I didn't mean to laugh. I just feel like we're finally starting to get somewhere, that's all. You know, as two grown men and not whoever we're pretending to be."

Another truck passed in the opposite lane. Steelcase. Big and dark blue. Like a rush of wind. It grated on Dan's already-shredded nerves.

"Got anything else you'd like to tell me?" Hapscomb said.

"When you ask the right questions, I guess we'll find out, won't we?"

Hapscomb laughed again, just a little this time. "Fair enough, Robertson. Fair enough."

The morgue was buried deep in the belly of Forest View Hospital, a clean, well-lit building that, based on its outward appearance, could've passed for an office complex. It was newer than anything in Ardor, with automatic sliding glass doors, a four-story concrete parking garage. A blanket of snow buried the sweeping, manicured grounds but they were nonetheless impressive.

After the detective flashed his badge at the front desk, signed in himself and a "guest," an attendant led Hapscomb and Dan straight through to the freezer, a cramped, gleaming stainless steel room. The floor was tile, a drain in its center. The frigid, deodorized air wasn't cold enough to cover up the formaldehyde smell, familiar from dissections in high-school science class.

Four large square doors were built into the wall, two only a few inches off the ground, the other two at waist-height. One of them had a small notecard tucked into a slot near the handle, scrawled with pen, "Lucas, Thomas." Dan did his best to ignore the notecard on the door right below it that read "Thompkins, Kenneth."

The hospital attendant cranked down on the handle of Tom's door and swung it open, pulled out a thin, steel-frame stretcher, like a massive oven pan, slid out on runners with a metal hiss and a click, snapping into place, Lucas's dead and bloodied body at Dan's feet like it was nothing that had ever lived, nothing that had ever been a threat—just nothing now and forever after.

He'd never known that Tom had a crude, blue-ink Tasmanian Devil tattoo on his chest, over his heart. And it seemed so fitting.

"Jesus," Dan said. He covered his mouth, didn't realize he was covering his mouth.

Back when they were kids, Tom and Dan, thirteen or fourteen years old, growing into themselves, their roles in town, that was when Tom had first emerged as a violent force in Dan's life, never letting him be, never letting him grow into a real person, feel good about himself. And Dan, he'd been so powerless, so helpless, unable to stand up for himself for as long as he could remember.

There was a girl, of course. There was always a girl. And her name was Vanderzane. Melissa Vanderzane. And she'd been so pretty. A pretty little redhead, pale skin stippled with brown blots of freckle. Dan couldn't help but be in love with her, not that he knew anything about love, and not that he'd ever worked up the nerve to talk to her. But Tom Lucas, big Tom Lucas, he was always laughing that big laugh, filling up the hallways with that laugh, stealing Melissa's homework and dangling it over her head, out of her reach, teasing her with his size, with his big laugh, and Melissa, she'd been so happy, always laughing, saying *Stop, Tom, just stop. You're so cruel.*

And then one day, after they'd dissected pig fetuses in science class, that formaldehyde smell still in his nostrils, trailing twenty or thirty feet behind her on her walk home from school, down those hilly tree-lined roads with their cracked sidewalks, Melissa had turned around and said, *Daniel? I know you're back there. You can come up and walk with me, you know.* He'd been so surprised to hear her voice saying his name, to realize that she was inviting him to be close to her, share her space, even more surprised when she took his hand in hers and said, *You know, I see the way you look at me. It's okay, you know. I think you're cute.*

Like something out of a dream. He started walking her home every day after school. She never took the bus and neither did he. Not when the weather was so nice, when those big bursting trees were so pretty and green, rustling in the wind. God, how he'd started feeling comfortable in his own skin. Too good to be true.

But because it was Dan Robertson, the quiet weirdo creep with the crazy sister, with the lottery-winning rich dad and that thing that happened at Silver Creek that no one ever talked about, because it was that guy who was walking pretty little redheaded and freckle-faced Melissa Vanderzane home, holding her hand and making her laugh with his quiet little voice, well, Tom Lucas had taken notice, and when Tom Lucas took notice, everyone else took notice, too. Sammy and Bill and some other flunkies and idiots—they'd all taken notice, all followed Tom as he followed Dan and Melissa on their way home from school, one brilliant and beautiful spring day, with the air all sweet and the sky all blue, had laughed and clapped their hands as Tom filled the air with his menace, with his insults and his threats. He wouldn't be ignored, couldn't be ignored. He was on them, tearing their hands apart, a big fist in Dan's eye smacking him to the ground, a big burst of pain and white shining stars like spiders spinning on strands of silk, Melissa crying out *Help me do something help me* and Dan's head spinning, Bill and Tom and the others hooting and hollering as Tom took the pretty little redhead right there on the side of the road, threw her down on the ground, kissing her, laughing. *What was he doing to her? What had he done?*

It had all been funny. But then Melissa's cries were so shrill and Tom had been so forceful, so red-faced and angry, that even Bill and Sammy and the others, they'd run off, scared. No one wanted to see that. No one wanted to interfere. And before he knew it, Tom was standing over Dan, pointing his big finger in Dan's face and saying, *You tell anyone and you're dead.* And he must've said the same thing to Melissa because, for whatever reason, as hard to believe as it might be, she never told a soul and the whole thing never came up again. Only as a memory, as a twisting and terrible dream that Dan saw again and again and again, helpless to stop it. Too weak to change what had been done.

Some memories haunt so strong, never leaving, permanent phantom smells.

"That's him," Dan said. He looked away from the corpse. "That's Tom Lucas."

"Ready to go on the record with that?"

Dan looked Hapscomb in the eye. "'Course I am. I'd know that motherfucker anywhere."

Hapscomb dropped Dan off at his mother's house.

Dan climbed the stairs, walked right on by her sick room, into his own room, and flopped belly-first onto the bed. The ride back from Forest Hills hadn't been any easier than the ride out. *You know that gun, the one you mentioned at the station yesterday, the one you said Tom said Kenneth used to kill himself? Well it still hasn't been found. Don't know anything about that, now, would you?* Dan's mind spinning, thinking. Trying to forget what Tom had said, hands bloodied from breaking out his living room window, *Bitches stole my gun... Lousy murdering fucks...* but bringing that up, couldn't be a good idea, would just raise more questions. Just remain silent. All Dan wanted at this point was to be left alone, to be uninvolved, to forget any of this mess had ever fallen into his lap. So then his mouth started flapping, *I told you I don't know anything. Never saw a gun. I only know what Tom told me...* And the lies just went on and on from there, spiraling like some out-of-control outer-space vortex swallowing up whole planets and stars. The spinning and the spiraling, perpetual.

Dan held onto his head and screamed into his pillow.

5

Early Afternoon, No Snowfall

Grace woke up naked, covered in a rough gray blanket, on the Newbert brothers' corduroy couch. The skin along her arms and legs itched something fierce. The lights were off, windows covered. A blue candle, melted to a small, crooked nub, burned on a large, flat stone in the corner of the room. The brothers made their own candles in lots of different colors, but they only burned blue ones when Grace was around, said it was for their own protection. The candle was the only light. No idea what time it was.

Her hands would not stop shaking. She lit a cigarette. It tasted terrible. She called out. No one was there. The brothers were gone, maybe. Today was the last day. She had a feeling somewhere deep in her twisted-up stomach that today was going to be the last day. Her head was all fucked up with terrible noises. Her head was pounding. Flipped the blanket back, turned on a nearby floor lamp.

Her arms and legs were covered with red welts. Itching like crazy. She'd forgotten that the brothers had bedbugs. Fuck. Those bites wouldn't disappear for weeks. But that didn't matter now.

It took a while, but she finally found some paper and a pen that worked. Had to search through piles of shit all over the floor, bloodied hunting knives, innumerable black t-shirts, porno magazines and spent shotgun shells. She blew out the stupid blue candle and curled back up on the couch and wrote the letter she'd been meaning to write forever, it seemed, scratching at her arms. Her head screamed with noises that weren't unlike her voice. She wrote. The words poured out of her.

Dear Dan,

By the time you read this I will have already done something terrible. But you left me with no choice and so I am writing you to explain to you how it is your fault that things have gotten so bad for me.

Everyone in Ardor has always pretended like my mother wasn't my mother, everyone always pretended like it was Bessie Robertson who birthed me, but we both know that is not the truth, that our selfish asshole father knocked up some scared little slut. I'm a whore's baby and that's all I've ever been.

When we were growing up, you were always so quick to tell people that I wasn't your real sister. And for a lot of years I really loved you for that because you were treating me like who I was, not pretending like I was someone else. It wasn't until later that I learned you were ashamed. That was the only real pain I ever remember feeling. It was like a tattoo I wore right on my face for everyone to see.

I guess it goes without saying that I hate our father. And that it's probably best he up and walked out on us after he won all that money. I hope that he dies soon too, that he drinks himself to death and shits out his guts and dies bloated and purple on the toilet. It will be a fitting end for him and I would love to dance something wild on his grave. You're always so quick to remind me that I have a daughter and let me tell you, I don't care that he is looking after her. I don't care about her either. She is just like him, selfish and a pig. They are a fit for each other.

How come you've never asked me about what happened at Silver Creek? Or where I was for all those days I was missing? How come you never asked me about Bicycle Bob? How come everyone in our family pretended like nothing ever happened? How come when I tried to tell you about The Worm, you told me I was crazy? Did you know that he raped me? Did you know that for years I couldn't remember that? Imagine coming to realize something like that in the dead of night.

God it is impossible for me to explain to you how much anger I have inside me and how badly I wish to hurt other people. I am filled with the ugliest black feelings and I've never known how to get rid of them.

Years back, when I was still in high school and just starting to act up, my mother found me. She lived one or two towns over and the guy she was shacked up with worked at Amway and apparently he came home from work one day telling her all these stories about some stuff I'd done with a bunch of guys at a party in Mecosta county. And so she called me and told me that she wanted to meet me and talk to me and hopefully set me straight in life. It turned out that for all those years we were growing up our dad was giving this bitch money, hundreds of dollars every month and now she wanted to give some of it to me.

Fox drove me out there one morning, to my mother's house, and the two of us sat down in her living room and before five minutes had gone by she was already rushing us out the door saying we were disrespectful and crazy and that we were devil worshippers and I struck her on the jaw and pulled her hair. She was an ugly woman who deserved to get hit. Hearing her scream made me feel better than I can tell you.

But like I said when I first started this letter, it is your fault that things have gotten so bad for me. Just like our father was giving that bitch money every month, I know he has been giving Bessie money every month too. And I know that you have it and that you've been saving it. You have never given me a dime. And when I came to your work yesterday and asked you to help me you said no. It never even crossed your mind that you might owe me everything you have, that if it hadn't been for me, you'd be dead now.

Or worse. You might be like me. You might be incapable of loving people because you got robbed of something inside you. Maybe you forgot what happened at Silver Creek but I sure as hell never did. My only consolation is that you are haunted by some of the same ghosts that haunt me.

We were there together. Remember that. But you went home long before I did.

You were my big brother. You were supposed to protect me. But you ran away and you hid. You stopped talking and closed yourself off to the big bad world but pretty soon, Daniel, there will be hell to pay. You will never live forever in the mouth of the mouth. You will never drink the blood of the Bornless One. You will never see outer space. You cannot hide from your own life. You are a pussy and a faggot. You cannot eat your own tail and disappear

*into nothingness. Not on today because this is the last day.
You will see. I am going to the river's end and I am giving
this whole town one last fuck you for good measure.*

    Grace

When she was done, she sealed the letter, got up and got
dressed. And then she was in her car and leaving Bolt
Street behind her, that disgusting trailer with its bedbugs
and its ghosts, behind her. Everything was behind her.
There was so much she had to do.

6

Afternoon, No Snowfall

Dan found the letter at the foot of the stairs. Grace's handwriting. He read it in the kitchen, sitting at the table, drinking his coffee. After that, he lost track of time for a while, staring off into space, processing things, hearing Grace's voice echoing in his head. *I need two thousand dollars... Fox is getting out in a few days...* Maybe things were more serious than he'd realized. He didn't know what to make of things. *Eating his own tail? Outer space? The river's end?* What did any of that even mean? All of these years and he'd never known how angry she really was on the inside. Maybe he could help change things. If it wasn't already too late. But where to start? Dan remembered Tupper's questions from the day before, asking about Grace and her connection to the Newbert Brothers. He'd heard plenty of talk of it before, gossip. Other people had asked him about it, what she was doing up there, that sort of thing. But he'd never gone up there to Bolt Street in his entire life.

He knew his search would have to start there.

It was the safest bet.

He slid open the big wooden door of the garage, climbed inside his mom's big old baby blue Cadillac. He hated driving. He never drove. But now he would have to. The engine turned over all tired and slow and cold. But it turned over, all the same. He looked at his watch. Not much longer and it would be getting dark. The trees would cast their long shadows into nighttime.

Bolt Street led to nowhere. And at its end, the Brothers' trailer, one of those silver-bullet things from the '60s, looking like a grounded zeppelin, a once-marvelous machine with the air taken out of it, now just some extension of this dirty and cracked little earth.

Dan met them out back, the Brothers—Lawrence and Teddy—standing on either side of a rusted-out garbage can, a bombed-out metal husk crackling with sparking orange and yellow flames, putting off a gray-green smoke, rippling the winter air. The Brothers both wore oil-stained and old, heavy flannels, their dirty bearded faces sucked with shadow, like black-eyed ghouls, burning skulls floating in that dirty damp yard. The hills on either side rose steeply, stuck with dead and scraggly tree trunks.

When he approached them, what was he expecting? He didn't know what to expect. He figured them to be nervous or scared or scary or maybe even violent. He had no idea, honestly. But whatever his expectations, he certainly hadn't been expecting them to be so friendly.

"You know who I am?" Dan said.

"Sure do," the bigger one said, the one with the tattooed knuckles wrapped around the neck of a beer bottle. "You're Grace's brother."

"Daniel," the other one said. "I'm Teddy." He nodded. "And this here's my brother Lawrence."

"You both know why I'm here?"

"Only two possible answers why, best I can figure," Lawrence said. "You're either here to score drugs or you're looking for Grace. That's the only two reasons anyone comes up here."

"I need to talk to her. I think she's in trouble."

"She ain't here," Teddy said. "But she were. Took off sometime this morning, didn't say nothing about where she was going. But I got some ideas."

"Will you—" Dan started.

"Out here at night," Lawrence said, looking at Dan across the fire, "it gets real dark, you know. Like really real."

"Like inside a cave," Teddy added.

"Okay, but—"

"And for some reason," Lawrence continued, "you can't ever see the stars. Not from these hills—never. It's like starlight don't reach these parts." He paused. "That's the blackness of the other side."

"Amen," Teddy said.

"What's this got to do with—"

"Your sister, she's got an evil inside her," Teddy said.

"Half-sister," Dan said. "She's not my—"

Teddy continued, "She's got the mark of the dark lord tattooed on the inside of her stomach." He nodded toward his brother. "We've both felt it there. Born of the blackness on the other side, beyond the mouth of the tunnel. The other world."

"We figured you should know that," Lawrence said. "So you can decide what to do."

"Right," Teddy said. "Because we'll tell you where she might be, but you're the one who's gotta decide whether or not she's worth saving."

"Might be better for everyone if you just let her burn out."

"Like a black star."

"Like a black star up in the sky."

Dan started noticing little things, things that made him nervous, like the way Lawrence's lips were moving even when he wasn't talking, or the way Teddy never seemed to blink, just staring wide-eyed like he didn't have any eyelids at all.

"It might be best," Teddy said, "if you let her burn herself up from the inside. *Ad astra et ultra.*"

"I just can't let myself do that," Dan said. He thought of the letter. "I owe it to her to try."

The fire cracked a pop and a big burst of blue flame hissed and lit up the inside of the can.

"Do you know what a grimoire is?" Teddy said.

"Black Grimoire," Lawrence added.

"No," Dan said.

"Oh," Teddy said. He shrugged a bit. "Nevermind then."

The fire crackled some more. Dan was losing his patience.

"Look, I'd sure appreciate it if you told me where I can find her."

The brothers exchanged a look, nodded, then turned back to Dan. Lawrence spoke first. "You know Fox's old place out by Deadguy Pond?"

7

Later Afternoon, No Snowfall

Surrounded by miles of unincorporated evergreen forest, Fox's cabin overlooked a steep hill that sloped down to Deadguy Pond. It was some fifteen minutes outside town.

Dan had been there once or twice when Grace had still been married to Fox. Drank beers with them in the unfinished basement. Even shot a game of pool or two with Fox, amazed that a guy that had been so popular in school was talking to a guy like him, like Dan Robertson, amazed that a guy like Fox had ever taken up with a girl like Grace.

It came back to him the way memories do—all on their own, unasked for. The way Fox would lean his hip on the pool table, keep one boot on the concrete floor, leaning on his elbow, tip of his pink tongue poking out the corner of his pursed lips, flannel sleeves rolled to his elbows. He was lining up a shot, sliding the cue back and forth between his two fingers. And then *clack*. The balls would be crossing all over the table, streaks of color, *clacking*. And another one would sink. And Fox would stand back with his arms crossed over his tight little gut, give Dan that look, his top lip pulled back in a smile, two front teeth visible, eyelids droopy with beer. *You're a loser, Robertson. Always have been. Always will be.*

Dan's mom's old Caddy skidded out a few times as he left County Road 9 and made his way up the curving driveway. He kept thinking about the Brothers. The creepy soundless movements of their mouths and the weird shit they actually said.

Pine trees surrounded him on both sides, as tall as he could see, their furry needles looking blue beneath the glare of the white sun.

He stopped the car fifty feet shy of the cabin, worried about someone hearing his approach. Got out and felt the cold air make his face go tight. Chirpings of cardinals and jays from the trees. The distant buzz of snowmobiles.

He started walking, put his hands in the pockets of his Carhartt. The sky was gray. Fox's narrow driveway was iced over, hard and slick like polished, gleaming stone. The crisp air bit at his nostrils with every breath, and his footsteps slid as he walked, boots searching for traction.

As he got closer, maybe 20 yards away, he was able to make out the muffled bass-heavy pulse of music—heavy metal. And then he saw the house.

It was a small place with bales of hay lining the north-facing foundation, windbreakers for those brutal winter months. The windows were covered with blue plastic tarps. The siding was unfinished, the color of burl. Hard-packed snow surrounded the cabin in sloping piles, as if the whole thing had been built into a bank.

He'd expected to find Grace here, but this music... She'd never listen to music like this: big and brutal, churning guitars, jackhammer drums, singing like barking, gnashing dogs.

Boots crunching in the snow, matching the pounding of his temples, Dan came up to the white, metal door, put his hand on the knob, felt its cold pinch his palm.

He opened the door. It screeched on its hinges.

The music engulfed him, like a wind. And then it was gone, dropped down to a murmur.

The first thing that took his attention was the smell, like skunked beer, dried vomit. The inside of the cabin was wood-paneled, the entire back wall floor-to-ceiling windows, overlooking Deadguy, blinding white, letting in a great blast of sunlight.

And in the center of the room, his legs wrapped up in a faded Care Bears sleeping bag, on top of a ratty throw rug, a kid. He was sitting up, his back against a rust-orange corduroy couch, strands of greasy black hair hanging over his eyes, chest bare and pale, big black boombox—top of the line—at his side.

"Who are you?" the kid said, voice trembling. He crossed his thin arms over his chest. Scar tissue on the inside of one his forearms, puffy white, all jagged like lettering, caught Dan's eye. A nasty cut. Could barely see it. "What the fuck are you doing here?"

Dan slammed the door behind him, looked around. Kitchen off to his right, totally trashed: open cartons of milk on the counter, fast food wrappers. Forests of empty beer bottles covered every available surface, the counters, the table, the stove.

The floor around the kid was littered with dirty clothes heaped in dark piles. The walls were bare. Some of the foam panels covering the ceiling had been pushed out of place, others sagged in the middle, nearly all of them were brown with water stains.

Place had changed since last time Dan set foot in it. Like a whirlwind come through, tore it all up. Had the mark of Grace all over it.

"Name Grace Robertson mean anything to you?" Dan said, taking a step into the room, kicking an empty can of beans with the toe of his boot, sending it skittering across the peeling linoleum of the kitchen.

The kid's Adam's apple dropped down, shot back up. Whatever he was about to say was a lie. "No. Never heard of her. Now who the fuck are you?" He brought his knees up to his chest, bundled under Lionheart, wrapped his arms around his knees. He was shaking. His arms were shaking, his eyes dead-looking.

"What are you, eighteen?" Dan said, taking another step forward. "Trying to intimidate me?" His breath was clouding in the air. They didn't have heat. But there was a Bunsen burner on the floor next to the kid—definitely not strong enough to heat a room.

Movement past the kitchen. Ten feet away, maybe. Peripheral. A girl, blonde hair, white skin. She emerged from the shadowy bedroom hallway. Grace.

But it wasn't Grace. Dan didn't know who it was. Her face was mousy, covered in red blotches. She wore an oversized sweatshirt and a pair of stonewashed jeans.

"I thought I heard you talking to someone," she said, addressing the kid, ignoring Dan. "Did he bring any shit?"

"Shut the fuck up," the kid said, snapping. And the girl's tiny hand clapped against her mouth. Her eyes wide. Like she'd just made a huge mistake.

"*Shit*?" Dan asked. "What d'you mean?" He looked at the kid. "What does she mean?"

The kid just sat there, stiff. His teeth were chattering. "You need to leave, dude. Seriously. You're totally freaking me out right now."

Dan turned back to the girl. "Who are—"

The girl spun on her heels, hair whipping, disappeared down the shadowy hallway. Dan heard a door slam back where Grace's bedroom used to be, cheap wood, more of a suck-shut than a slam.

"*Dude?*" Dan asked, back to the kid, taking another step forward.

The kid flinched, his eyelids flicked shut, open. A glimpse of his teeth between his chapped lips, yellowed. Meth teeth. He tucked a strand of his black hair behind his ear, hand still shaking.

"The name Grace Robertson *mean* anything to you?" Dan repeated.

"Fuck," the kid muttered, "I already told you—"

"You didn't tell me shit."

"—I never heard a'her."

"Bullshit." Dan was standing a foot or two in front of the kid, towering over him, hands balled at his sides. Now his own hands were shaking. Shit, it was cold in here. Breath coming out in clouds. Light off Deadguy hitting the back of his skull.

The kid's arm shot out at his side—Dan nearly jumped out of his skin—and flicked on a small metal knob on the side of the Bunsen burner. There was a hiss and the *fwoom* of the blue flame as it bloomed into a needle-thin point.

"Fuck."

"Just relax," the kid said, words spilling out of his mouth. "You wanna come in here be a hardass, take our shit, kill us, I don't fuckin' know, fine, fuck you then, but I'm getting high then and you can't say fuck all."

Dan got down on one knee, eye to eye with the kid. He pointed at the kid's face. "You know whose place this is?"

"You cops?"

Dan shook his head. "Do I look like cops?"

"Then what the fuck you care? Fuck yeah I know whose place this is. Fuckin' Fox Peterson."

"He know you're here?"

"How the fuck I'm supposed to know? He's up in Ryan, outside Detroit. I don't get the feeling he knows much a'anything goes on around here no more."

"But he's getting out in a few days."

The kid shrugged, didn't seem to have heard, or didn't care either way. He twisted his torso, turned away from Dan, pale white stomach sucking up against his spine, skinny as all hell, leaned forward and grabbed something off the floor. A glint in the light. A knife.

Dan grabbed the kid's bicep closest to him, ice cold, like a dead guy, closed his hand around it, squeezed as hard he could. "No." Sounded calmer than he would have expected.

The kid yelped, arched his back, stomach heaving in and out, a burst of breath. His voice cracked. He held the knife up in the air, lying flat in his open palm. A butter knife: its tip charred to shit, blackened.

"Let go of me, motherfucker," the kid said, wrenching his arm free from Dan's grip. "I fuckin' told you, I'm getting high. I'm not gonna try anything."

Dan licked his lips. Didn't know what move to make. The skin on the kid's arm, the skin where he'd squeezed him, was white as snow. The color—*what color?*—slow to come back.

"Come on, get high with me. Chill out."

The kid tucked his hair behind his ear again, anger seemed to slide away, just like that, like snapping your fingers, his face slack like nothing happened, like Dan never grabbed him or nothing.

"I'm down to resin," he said, twisting around again. "No meth," he said. "But it's okay 'cause there's some crack resin mixed in it. It'll get you nice and fucked up." He came back with a second butter knife, also blackened. He laid them down on the carpet next to the hissing burner. "We're doing knives." His eyes flicked up, met Dan's. Dan's skin crawled.

Grace. She'd been here. He could feel it. Could almost smell it. The disarray, the mess. This kid. The girl. All of it. Exactly the kind of trail she'd leave. A mess.

Grace. Gone again.

Grace. What would she do? She'd say *Yeah, fuck yeah.*

Why did Grace do the things that Grace did? He never could figure her out. What was it they'd said? She had the mark of the lord tattooed on the inside of her stomach? Jesus. A bad seed. A bad girl. One of the bad girls. Liked to fuck. Let guys fuck her all the time all through high school all the time. Town bicycle. Haha.

This mess. This kid.

Dan nodded his head. "I'm in," he said. And everything inside him knotted up and he forgot he was cold for a second. He felt his heart beat in his throat.

The kid had a straightened paper clip between his thumb and his pointer finger, was scraping out the bowl of a little metal pipe, working at it real delicate-like, like he was gluing model pieces together, model engine parts in a model car.

He smeared the clump of what looked like tar on one of the butter knives.

We're doing knives.

Licked his lips again and thought about telling the kid he'd never done this before, that he'd never smoked anything really, especially never gotten high. But then he thought no, that it didn't matter. This would bring him closer to Grace. This would let him know, for a few moments at least, what it was like. Didn't he owe that to her?

"What's your name?" Dan asked. He got down on both knees now, wedged his hands between his thighs.

"Kenneth."

"What's your last name, Kenneth?"

The kid acted like he didn't hear. He held one of the knives—the one without the resin on it—over the burner flame.

"Who's the girl, Kenneth?"

"My sister."

The tip of the knife was glowing orange.

"Here." Kenneth held a Gatorade bottle, its bottom cut off, all rough, cut with scissors, holding it out to Dan.

Dan took the Gatorade bottle.

"The knife is hot." He *knew*, knew Dan had never done this. He was explaining. He was explaining how to do it. "Put the lip of the bottle up to your mouth, yeah like that, like it's a bong, get ready. Get over the knife. Make sure the plastic don't touch the knife otherwise you'll get a lungful of melted plastic."

He took the hot knife off the flame, held it in his right hand, still glowing orange, held the knife with the resin on it in his left hand. He pressed down on the resin with the hot knife. Held them together, crossed, like an X. Smoke shot up into the air like a goddamned geyser.

"Get over it. Now. Yeah, like that. Inhale. Not just in your mouth. Pull the air down into your lungs. Like use your stomach and breathe in deep. Yeah, like that. Take in as much as you can. Slowly... Slowly... Hold it in. Keep holding it."

Dan's cheeks were all puffed out. His throat was on fire, chest on fire. *Holy shit.* Tasted like ammonia at the back of his mouth, the smell of freshly laid tar. Stinging somewhere in his chest.

He wavered on his knees, fell forward onto his hands, crunched the Gatorade bottle on the floor beneath his hand, heard it crinkle, smoke pouring out his mouth like he was puking, felt like he was puking, eyes blurry with hot tears and there was no air, he tried to breathe but there wasn't any air. His whole body tensed and he heaved, coughed.

"Shit, dude," Kenneth said, slapping Dan on the back, on his jacket, goddamn he still had his jacket on. "Slower next time, that was too fast. I told you slow."

Dan could barely hear the kid's voice. Rush of water in his ears. The white light off Deadguy. Cold like a dead guy. And then a warm vibration like a radiator kicking on. All the colors of the room brighter. The white light off Deadguy cold like a dead guy. The textures all blurry.

He coughed again, straining his throat, an upper-respiratory-infection-cough and bam just like that it hit him he was high high as fuck.

The kid was laughing like a weasel. Like a fox. *Fucking Fox Peterson.* Slapped Dan on the back again. Or still the feeling from the first time. Already had the knife back over the flame, getting it hot again. His turn now.

"You ever hear of a band called Deicide?" the kid asked.

Deicide. What the fuck's that word mean? Dee-uh. Dee-uh-side.

"Death metal," the kid said. "From Florida. Where it's warm and shit—not like fucking dickbone Michigan. All the best bands live in Florida. It's fucking awesome there."

He reached over and pushed a button on the boombox. Dan was still coughing, still heaving, like he'd never breathe again.

There was a noise, the speakers pulsing, an incredibly loud noise, the sound of a metal door, a prison door, slamming shut *clang* and then the music, same music Dan had heard from outside, from the driveway, filling the room like a jackhammer: big and brutal, churning guitars, thick drums, and then the lyrics like barking, gnashing dogs. Drums pounding impossibly fast in a static rhythm, pounding like a jackhammer, blasting. Growls like demons.

The kid had the Gatorade bottle held between his lips, held the knives in a cross, yellowish smoke shooting up the bottle, straight down his throat. And then he dropped everything, eyelids half-shut, leaned back against the orange couch, shot the smoke straight up in the air in a controlled stream, looked back at Dan and opened his mouth and said something but Dan couldn't hear what, not over the music, it was too loud, didn't hear what the kid said but it looked like he said fuck or fuck yeah or something like that.

Dan's coughing was calming down. He was breathing again, breathing normal. He sat cross-legged, across from Kenneth, the burner between them, still burning that blue-tipped needle-thin point.

The kid was on his feet, still had the scorched butter knives in his hands, one in each hand. He was just skin and bones, wearing nothing but a pair of black silk boxer shorts, little legs like a chicken, big bruises all over, looking like a birch tree. Dan saw bruises like this on kids before, snowboarders had them, hockey players, kids that were used to falling on hard surfaces, kids that lived rough.

Dan looked up at the sagging, dripping ceiling panels all brown and nasty and the words *rough housing* spun around his mind in a circle like carved-wood horses painted up bright on a carousel, spinning round and round, *rough housing rough housing rough housing rough housing* and god damn he was laughing so hard he couldn't see through the tears in his eyes and his jaw started aching something awful, *rough housing rough housing rough housing.*

"Dude," Kenneth said, yelling, "you're high as fuck." He was smiling, eyes glassy, milky yellow. "Here, take these, get ready to go again." He handed the butter knives over to Dan. Dan took them in one hand.

The kid slapped his knee, a little weasley laugh. Started yelling again. "Wait. Come here, I want to show you something cool." He pointed down to the floor, lipped the word *basement.*

The kid turned around, walked to the back of the room by the windows, big windows overlooking Deadguy.

Dan climbed to his feet, followed, dragged the Care Bears sleeping bag along with the tip of his boot for a step or two, forgot it was there, shook it off. He was still laughing, his shoulders bouncing up and down, jaw still aching, knives cold in his hand. He wiped his eyes with the back of his jacket sleeve, shook his head back and forth.

Kenneth was at the top of the stairs leading down into the basement. He turned and waved Dan to keep following, mouthed something again.

Dan still couldn't hear. Jackhammer drums pounding. He could feel it in his chest, could feel how old his knees felt walking down those stairs, one at a time, after kneeling on the floor for so long.

Not so young anymore. Feeling it. You never think about it and then you feel it and you know you know like it's something new.

Kenneth flicked on the lights. Rectangular panels of harsh fluorescents, one in each corner of the room, flickered a bit, then hummed evenly. White light like the reflections off Deadguy.

The basement was still unfinished: concrete floor, copper piping snaking along the ceiling, walls tarped in clear plastic, no insulation, exposed 2x4s running floor-to-ceiling, spaced evenly—a foot apart—the vinyl-topped bar against the corner nearest the stairs in the shape of an L.

Two sliding glass doors on the far side of the room gave way to the sloping, icy back yard, sloping all the way down to Deadguy.

The sun was going down. Gray clouds in the sky were starting to purple. It was getting late. Four. Maybe four-thirty.

And in the center of the room—exactly like he remembered it—was Fox's regulation-size pool table; the felt was as green as any golf course Dan had seen on television, pristine. The balls were racked, cue ball in the center of the table, a nine-ball game ready to go.

The music upstairs was thudding through the ceiling, slightly muffled, but still loud as all hell.

"Come here," the kid said, looking over his shoulder again, waving again, "it's back here."

"That girl upstairs was your sister?" Dan asked, boots clopping against the concrete.

"It's back here." Kid wasn't listening. He went behind the vinyl-topped bar, turned sideways slid through the space between the bar and the plastic-tarp wall. "You're gonna love this thing, I show everyone who comes over. It's amazing." He ducked down, out of sight.

Dan slapped the butter knives onto the bar, leaned onto his elbows, stood up on his tiptoes, peered over the other side.

The kid was squatting, bony knees jutting out at his sides, squatting next to a three-foot-tall stuffed bird—an emu.

He had his arms wrapped around its body like he was posing for a picture with it and he was looking back at Dan with pride flashing in his eyes, yellow teeth flashing between those chapped lips.

The bird's head was the size of a tennis ball, covered in black feathers, sharp gray beak; a patch of blue-green flowing down into the light brown feathers of the neck, nearly a foot long, thick as Dan's forearm. The rest of the bird was built like a loaf of bread, like a single-humped camel or something, covered in brown and tan feathers, parallel with the ground. And its legs, its legs looked like dinosaur legs, scaly rough skin the color of mud, feet like chicken claws.

Fox had a thing for birds. Fuck, nearly forgot that. Budding bird watcher always talked about the way they flew, how the hawks never had to flap their wings, how they could just glide.

"You knew Fox?" Dan asked.

The kid smiled even wider. "Fuck yeah I knew Fox. Everyone knew Fox, man. Fox is the only reason anyone in this shithole town knows anyone."

"And that's his bird?" Dan pointed at the emu with two of his fingers, thumb straight up in the air, hand in the shape of a gun, he pointed at the bird.

112

"Bought it right before he got sent up," Kid Kenneth said, nodding. "Always talked about how it was his prized possession. How he'd have a whole room full of 'em once he got enough money together. Better than putting money in a bank." He turned back to the bird, shifted on his feet and rubbed his cheek against the puffy feathers along its chest. He turned back to Dan. "Said this fucker was worth a ton of money. At least a couple hundred bucks. Grace thinks we can get two-fifty if we find the right buyer."

Dan heard the name and it took him a few seconds to realize that he'd heard it. In that time the pounding music thudding through the floor found a rhythm with his heartbeat and he felt his whole body go hot.

He remembered the way the kid's Adam's apple had bounced up and down. When he'd asked him if he knew Grace Robertson. If that name *meant* anything.

And then he took another look at those scars on the kid's arm. The jagged lettering. Spelled out *SLAYER*. And he remembered where he'd heard that word—from Nancy Van Horton. Talking about Kenneth's kids. Kenneth Thompkins. *Left two kids behind. Those kids are wild.*

Dan licked his lips, snatched the knives up off the bar.

The kid never even saw him coming, still just squatting there, stoned, his stick-thin arms draped around the stuffed bird.

But he was there, around the bar, and on the kid, all in a matter of moments, a few seconds, a few heartbeats.

Screaming.

The emu toppled over, the sound of flesh hitting concrete.

The kid thrashed as Dan pinned him to the floor, straddled his chest. He let his knees come down on the kid's shoulders, could feel the bones grind into the concrete—he must've had seventy, eighty pounds on him.

He wrapped his left hand around Kenneth's throat, dug the tip of one of the charred butter knives into the kid's forehead with his right hand, pressed down with his thumb, knuckle turning white, putting on the pressure.

The kid howled, grit his teeth, jut his chin into the air, neck muscles strained and stringy, still thrashing, fighting, like he was having seizures.

Kenneth's neck felt slick against Dan's hand, sweating, slippery, hot

He'd never done anything like this before, had never done anything so violent. He squeezed the kid's neck tighter. Imagined the trachea pinching shut. He put more pressure on the butter knife with his thumb and the kid howled again.

Jesus God he was angry, had never been this angry before, and he wanted to hurt this kid real bad, wanted to hurt him like he'd never hurt anyone before. He wanted to split the fucker's head open right there on the floor. The smack of flesh on concrete. Legs thrashing everywhere. Screaming. The pounding thudding jackhammer music. Possessed dogs from hell. Pristine green. *You're a loser, Robertson. Always have been. Always will be.*

"You lied to me, motherfucker."

Slammed the kid's head into the floor, a sick thud. A thick thud.

Kid was crying, crying out loud, screaming.

And then Dan heard the quick thump-thump-thump-thumping of the girl coming down the stairs, running down the stairs. He knew it was her before he even saw her, nearly expected her after the kid started screaming like a fucking—

He barely had time to look over his shoulder before she leapt onto his back and wrapped her arms around his neck, screaming in his ear, terrified.

Dan let go of the knife, heard it go clattering onto the concrete, and the kid scrambled into the corner where the bar met the wall, the clear tarp wall, curled up into a ball and moaning, slobbering.

The girl was still screaming and Dan rose to his feet with her still trying to choke him, the crook of her arm squeezing around his throat, using her other arm for leverage. "Get the fuck offa me." And he threw his shoulder forward, felt her slide over him and smack the floor hard on her hip.

He caught a glimpse of that blotchy red face before he turned and stormed out from behind the bar, hitting his shoulder hard trying to squeeze through that narrow space, hitting his shoulder on the bar. He stormed across the room, boots clomping, slid open that glass sliding door, out into the icy sloping backyard.

Away from that jackhammer music, from those kids, and my God did that kid really say his name was *Kenneth*? And that that girl was his *sister*? How had he not realized? The image of those work boots sticking straight up through the ice. The boat launch. How had this all happened so quickly?

The sky arced over him like a big crinkly garbage bag poked with little holes letting in light. Head pounding even harder now.

Scrambling on the snow, his feet slipped forward out from beneath him, dropped him right on his ass, hard, and he slid downward to the bottom of the hill where the ice leveled out. Scrambling again, ass throbbing with pain, legs tight with strain, boots sliding and slipping. And he knew he was out on Deadguy, that Deadguy was frozen over and he was running out on the ice, out into the middle of the pond where there was nothing, nothing at all, no jackhammer music, no devil dogs, no little girls with blotchy red faces and meth teeth. None of that and none of nothing.

Felt nearly like one of his lungs burst and Dan skittered to a halt on the ice, slipped and came down hard on his thigh and his elbow, bare hand freezing against the ice.

He lay on his back, world spinning around him, ice cool on the back of his head, hands out at his sides. He lay there and he breathed. Focused on his breathing. The stars like little holes poked in the garbage bag sky. Fucking trash floating around inside. And he thought about what Grace had written in her letter, about how he would never see outer space, all that empty black and forever cold.

And he screamed as loud as he could into the sky, not caring if any of the cottages around him had their lights on, little orange lights glowing in the dark, not caring if anyone heard him at all, probably better if they did because at least then someone would know he was feeling something that was too big, too hard, too tough for words.

Day Three

1

Early Morning, Light Snowfall

Nancy drove her little Tercel up a winding hill and let out the clutch as she coasted down the other side, gliding smooth and controlled over the frozen dirt, muffler cutting, a silent glide, big patches of icy fields glinting and glaring beyond the thin tree-line, everything all dead and mangled and just so goddamned depressing.

Winter takes its toll on a person, Nancy thought. Sure, some of that can be justified, like yeah, she suffered from Seasonal Affective Disorder (and what an acronym!) but really, everyone in the world is sad, everyone wakes up in the morning and wonders what the fuck is going on, or why the world is so big and scary—not to mention cold—but the northern person, the person born with cold in their soul, the truth is, well, they're stronger than most folks because they're used to toughing it out, they're used to waking up early, when it's still black outside, heating up a pot of water on the stove, lugging it outside and using it to unfreeze the locks of their car. They're used to the slow turnover of a cold engine, the slow wait for the windows to defrost, the bite of the cold steering wheel in the soft skin of their palms. That's what life in Michigan is all about—toughing it out. And waiting. Waiting for the ice to thaw, waiting for the days to grow long, for the trees to come alive, the buds to bloom. It's just the way it is. And even when things warm up and the sun burns through the tinfoil clouds, the northern person is just counting the days before winter rears its ugly gray skull, once more and forever always, comes down from the sky like the world's wettest blanket, muffling the summer sounds, a slick surface for the wind to whittle its sharpness to a point, its bone-baring whistle.

The clutch popped back into second, then third as she climbed another hill, muffler blaring. So easy to get distracted when you're driving, lost in thought.

And then up the road, shuffling along with a limp, jacket iced-over, what are the odds—Dan Robertson. Twice in just a few days. And at this hour, Jesus Christ. Her muffler roaring as she trucked closer, Dan glanced over his shoulder, took a high step into the snow bank on the side of the road and threw a hand up in the air, a bare hand, the man wasn't even wearing gloves. Nancy put pressure on the brakes nice and slow, slid to a nice slow halt. Dan's face was grim. He looked half-frozen, drained of color, tinged blue. He got in, shivering so hard it was like he was having a seizure, his breathing all raspy and jagged, hair all full of snowflakes melting into heavy fat drops as the dash heat hit hard.

"Jesus, Dan, you must be freezing. What the hell are you—"

"I can't...please...just take me...home."

Nancy didn't ask any questions, just drove. "Jesus," she said again and didn't even hear it, never thought about why. She knew something bad had happened, could feel it, really. Dan was like a blackness. And combined with the

119

visit from the detective the day before, it all added up to a big fat sum of bad, a swollen storm-cloud out in the distance. She didn't have to ask questions, didn't want to interfere. And by the time she got her little car into second gear she'd already made the decision to call Hapscomb as soon as she got the chance.

Dan leaned forward with his hands on his knees, inspecting the side door of his mother's farmhouse. Two deep gouges cut through the white paint near the dead bolt. A black smudge of a boot-print alongside the handle. Dan leaned down with his hands on his knees and ran two fingers along the gouges, barely grazing, and still the door creaked open a bit, leading into the kitchen. The gouges were thick, had ribbed the wood. A crowbar.

Nancy stood a few steps behind him in the snowed-over walkway. "What is it? Is something the matter?"

Dan stood straight and pushed the door all the way open. "Looks like someone broke in last night." Didn't even turn to look at her, his chin on his chest, shame pumping through his head. He'd dropped his guard. He'd left the house for an entire night. Had left her alone.

He went inside and rushed up the stairs.

Nancy followed, watched Dan as he reached the top of the stairs, turned round the banister, went out of sight, heard a door open, smack against the wall.

There was mud on the stairs—and not fresh mud neither. Dried to a crust. Nancy looked around, looked for a phone, and saw one mounted on the wall through the doorway and into the kitchen. She went to it, already reaching into her purse to pull out her pocketbook, to find Hapscomb's card, and passed the living room, saw the floor covered in smears of what looked like mud, glass everywhere, a garbage bag taped over a broken window. Something had happened here, something violent. And for the first time, Nancy realized that things were happening all around her, right at that moment, things that she couldn't understand and probably wouldn't want to understand.

As she hung up, she heard Dan's heavy slow footfalls lumbering down the stairs, painfully slow. He was sobbing or moaning or something like that. She stood at the foot of the stairs, one hand up on the railing, the other over her mouth, watching a grown man cry, what are you supposed to say? Are you supposed to give him a hug or what? "Dan," she said, "what's wrong? What's happened?"

Dan was curled up on the top step, his arms crossed over his knees, head tucked away, rocking back and forth. The whimpering. Jesus. It was a brutal sound. And a grown man. A grown man should never cry like that. Completely out of control and unrestrained. She gripped the rail, imagined her fingernails cutting into the wood.

"What's happened?" she said, again, her voice like fingernails this time, cutting.

Dan looked up, his eyes all red and watery, lower lip trembling like a baby. "She's dead."

"Who's dead?" She took a step, didn't even realize she was taking a step.

"My mom. She's dead. I left her… I left her alone and now she's dead." His hands went to his stomach, like a woman caressing her pregnant belly. "The doc said, said that there's a good chance I'll have it, too."

Another step. "Calm down. One thing at a time. Take a deep breath. There. That's good. Now another one. Okay. Tell me what happened."

He was curled up again, sobbing into his arms, still wearing his jacket. "She was here. My sister was here. She took everything—the pills, the drugs, all the money. She took everything."

Jesus, the stairs were just filthy with mud. And then the smell hit her. A thick and ripe smell. She couldn't help but wonder when was the last time someone cracked a window around here. This house was positively rank, air as thick as baking bread, and the thought made her sick to her stomach, flooded her mouth with saliva, with mucus. The way Dan held his stomach. What was he talking about? *The doc?* It made her feel so, so sick. She couldn't take another step. Couldn't get any closer to that blubbery mess of a man, couldn't back down the stairs, either. What if he took it the wrong way? She closed her eyes and breathed through her mouth. Just listened. To the sobbing. The sobbing. Like so much running water. Jesus.

The ugliness of northern life, it sometimes seemed to Nancy, was everywhere. In the trees, the cloud-crowded skies, the waters.

Like the Thornapple. Such an ugly river. With its opaque brown waters, and its ugly name, dumping its runoff into bigger, stronger streams, or else into the unending mazes of creeks of backwater sinkholes, towns filled with tight-lipped ghosts, snow-frozen souls.

Its waters are only fit to fill the steaming sewers of mid-sized towns, or Michigan's cold and prim sleeping cities, concrete centers that the rest of the world has long put out of mind.

The Thornapple's winding body and its non-navigable waters, bringing nothing to nobody. A steady stream of pointlessness. A withered worm in a rotten apple. A river surrounded by a stillness, whose muddy banks go untrodden, whose tireless, repressed rage goes unheard, out of earshot, trembling with inarticulate anger.

They were angsty thoughts, teenage thoughts, the words of better-forgotten poems her students might scratch into their notebooks. But they were also the truth, her own truth.

Somewhere it continues.

2

Early Afternoon, Light Snowfall

When Grace came back for Kenneth Jr., he was freaking out, shaking, pacing, unable to sit down for like more than thirty seconds before he was back up on his feet, shaking, pacing. His forehead was smudged with soot—she couldn't believe Dan had such aggression in him—and bruised a bit. His eyes were pink and swollen. From crying? The skin around his knuckles was all raw, dusted white, and Grace guessed that he'd been down in the basement, taking out his aggression on the drywall, taking out his fear or his hurt, taking something out. It wouldn't have been the first time. Jesus, what the hell had happened here? She'd only left for one night and—

"You said we were gonna go to Florida," Kenneth said, lowering his voice, trying to sound tough, and dammit if his voice didn't crack. Grace had to swallow a laugh. "You said that after we got some money together we were gonna take off and never have to see this fucking dickbone town ever again." He turned to Grace, suddenly stopped his pacing, pointed at her, said "You lied to us," as he stabbed his finger at her, stabbed as he said each word.

They were in the kitchen, the three of them, beneath the buzzing lights, Grace and Kenneth Jr. and Kenneth's sister, Kendra. And while Kenneth was freaking out, Grace sucked down a cigarette, picking up random bottles of beer, looking for one with a little bit left, with a mouthful or,

God willing, maybe one that had been left unopened. But there wasn't anything left around this place. It had been drained dry.

"Listen," she said, slamming an empty bottle down on the counter, that glass-pop sound, "I never said we weren't going to Florida, so just calm down. I just said that, well, when I asked you why my mother's car was parked down at the road, I asked you what happened, and, when you told me, I just said that we were going to have to deal with one more thing before we could go."

Kendra sat up on the counter next to the microwave, her legs dangling, crossed at the ankles, arms folded over his stomach. The girl's posture was something sad, all hunched, arching backbone. Shape of a question mark. Her whole being was a question mark. Clueless. She kept her face down, hiding behind her bangs. "You're a liar," she said, or barely said, more of a mumble. She looked up. Tough little girl. Her eyes were wet, her makeup a mess. "My brother's right. And after all we done. After all we done for you."

Grace stared unblinking at the girl until the girl looked away, hid behind her bangs again. Not so tough after all. She then turned back to Kenneth. "We're still going to Florida. There's just one last thing we have to do—and I need both of you to help me." She paused. Thought about what to say. "This is the most important part. If we don't do this, then everything, everything we've done so far, none of it will matter. Do you understand me?"

"Why should we trust you?" Kenneth said. And he was so goddamn sincere, his eyes were so goddamn wide, that

Grace knew she was losing him, that she was losing both of them, losing their confidence, their trust. "We already done everything for you. We sold drugs for you. We made money for you. We took care of our dad for you, we—"

"Listen," Grace said, "that wasn't my fault. Your dad…" Kendra looked up again, some terrible awful look on her face, like one of those sad clowns you see in velvet paintings. "I don't got nothing to say about your dad," she said, doing her best not to look at that girl's terrible face. "But he threatened all three of us—threatened all our hard work. Don't you get it? If we'd given him what he wanted, we'd never, ever make it down South. He'd just keep asking for more. He'd never let us be, 'cause he knew too much." Kendra back behind her bangs. Kenneth still staring hard. "And that's why he had to go."

Kendra whimpered a little. Kenneth looked straight up at the ceiling and sighed, exhaled loudly. His face was all crumpled up like he was holding back tears.

"It's more important than ever now that we get movin'," Grace said. "The fact that my brother was here, that's not good." She made eye contact with Kenneth. "And I don't know what happened between him and you but he'll be coming back. I know him."

Silence. Grace looked to Kenneth, to Kendra. They both avoided her eyes. They were both scared, clearly. Scared little children. And she would have to be the one to take care of them, shelter them. There was only one way she knew how to do that, to truly save them from their pain, remove them from their hurt.

"Tom Lucas is dead," Grace said. "I just heard earlier today. It's a gift. So now there ain't nothing that no one can trace back to us. We need to go now. There's never been a better time."

"Where were you last night?" Kenneth said. He hadn't even been listening, all wrapped up in his thoughts. His voice was all kid-like again.

Grace knew she could still save them, could still save the trust they had in her. She saw that now. These kids had no one. They had nothing. They needed her. And she needed them to need her. It made her feel full.

"I already told you," she said, softening, "I was getting the money we needed. And I got it—it's out in my car right now. So pack up your stuff—only take what you need. We gotta go right now. I'll tell you everything you need to know once we hit the road."

Silver Creek. Down by the big sewer grate. I guess that's where it all started. I'd followed my brother down there one day. An overcast sky, I think. Or maybe we'd gone down there together. I can't remember. I can't imagine why we'd go down there. All our lives, we'd heard that place was haunted by perverts and drifters. Our parents had always told us to stay away, that it wasn't safe, of course that's where we'd go to play. We wanted to see what was so scary about it, what all the fuss was about, I guess. I mean, I was all of six years old. I didn't know much of anything, you know what I mean? I was just following my

*big brother. And he was supposed to keep me safe. He was
my protector. Supposed to be.*

*You both know about Bicycle Bob, right? The freak?
That ain't no legend. That's the goddamned truth. He's a
real person. He used to live near town, by Gaslight Avenue.
That terrible old blue house with the sagging old rotten
porch. All the kids used to tell stories about him. About how
he had kids chained up in his basement. He'd make those
kids drink water out of dog bowls. Just horrible stuff. The
worst kind of stories. They said he never had a childhood,
that he was born a full-grown man. That he lived in that
house since forever.*

*But he was real. Bicycle Bob. And he was down there,
in the sewer, hiding in the dark, his face painted up like the
Wicked Witch of the West from the Wizard of Oz, all green
and long and big black eyebrows. That face used to terrify
me when I was a kid, when that movie would come on TV.
And. And we were lost in those dark cement pipes. I think.
Dan and me. It was like a maze filled with screaming. And
Bob was grabbing at us with his big hands, so soft, like
pillows. And the next thing I remember Bob had a knife and
Dan was yelling and Bob slashed at Dan with the knife and
cut Dan's shoulder open something real bad. Dan was
bleeding everywhere. Dan ran out of there and left me
behind. And then I was facedown in the water. There was
like a little stream of water running through the pipe. And
Bob was holding me down. I had grit between my teeth.
Bicycle Bob was talking so fast. I couldn't make out any of
his words. He was just blubbering out sounds like a deaf
child having a tantrum. Then I could breathe again. Bicycle*

Bob's voice had fallen to a whisper, right in my ear. He was holding me tight. Rocking me. He told me all about The Worm. And how the inside of The Worm's stomach is larger than our entire universe, filled with ever-expanding space—beyond time. No one ever gets hurt inside its stomach. There's no pain. There's only floating and like painlessness. And everyone lives forever in bliss.

He told me how The Worm needs to be fed. That's exactly what he said. The Worm needs to be fed to be happy. Otherwise it's sad and no one is safe.

And then he put the worm in me.

And then everything was dark for a while.

I don't know what happened after that. One day I just realized that I was back home. My dad, he was still around then, he found me in our front yard, I think. That's what he told me. I don't remember anything. They told me that I'd been gone for days. Dan couldn't look me in the eye. He went weird from that day on. Was never the same kid. Everyone was so worried about him. No one ever thought that maybe something bad had happened to me. I'd just been missing. No one ever asked me what happened. No one could look me in the eye. Everyone just went weird from that day forward. Weird in the worst way.

Minutes Earlier, Light Snowfall

Hapscomb had just gotten back from the Ryan Correctional Facility, taken 96 all the way back—a straight shot. He was tired. His nerves were on edge. And so he'd jumped when the phone rang.

"This is," he said. Listened. "That's exactly who I want to see. I'll be over in no time. Just stay put. Don't let him go anywhere."

He hung up the phone. Everything was coming together.

Afternoon, No Snowfall

Grace heard The Worm's cries in the distance as she drove, the heavy breathing as it shuffled through the underground, from one chamber to the next, filling the sewer pipes with its massive body. The howl of hunger. She laughed to herself. The Worm was always hungry. She imagined a vast blackness, a grid of bright green lines, afloat atop the billowing black, the vectors flexing, bending, never breaking, and then there in the distance, a great gaping gash, a wormhole tearing through textured tissue, a cone, a siphon of downward-suck, pulling space inside itself. Time pulling inside itself, a new fold, a hidden fold, forever-forgotten. The Worm was always hungry. She would feed The Worm. The green lines fell away from the fold. There was only blackness, rumpled and awash. There were no lines. There was no distance. Grace wasn't laughing anymore. There was no laughter. What marvelous things she would see. Entire worlds of a pure and singular color. A color beyond human vision. Kingdoms built inside iridescent bubbles. New kinds of horses. She was so used to hearing the laughing, the laughter all around her, coming from the woods at night. How deep these new oceans would be, she couldn't imagine. Deep enough to fall into. Underwater forests and eyeless glowing fish and giant whales swallowing whole beams of light as tall as the buildings in New York. And what's that in the distance? A red fissure between two crags of blackened rock, like a flap of flesh, endless inferno. The eye. There was light at the bottom of the ocean and it scared her. Grace was driving into the distance. There was nothing in the distance. There were kids in her car. There was trust in her car. She thought, maybe, she was doing the wrong thing. For just a second. That she should stop. But then she heard The Worm's hunger howl. And she laughed so hard she almost lost control.

5

Afternoon, Light Snowfall

When Hapscomb entered the Robertson farmhouse, he recognized the smell of death instantly. He knew what had happened, knew it instantly, felt it, knew that Dan's mother was dead, and a strange feeling of guilt washed through him. He would only be making this man's life tougher in the next few hours, in the next few days, however long it took until things were put right again. But that was his job. It was nothing personal. He had to repeat that to himself. It was nothing personal.

He shut the door behind him.

Nancy met him in the hallway, explained, in hushed words, what he already knew to be true. Bessie was dead, she said. Dan's mother was gone.

She led him back to the kitchen, pointed out the broken window and the destroyed room, just in case he needed to know. Hapscomb didn't react. Not visibly.

Dan sat at the table, a mug of coffee steaming before him, untouched. He greeted the detective with a nod. The lights were off and blue-white light was everywhere, a layer of ice on everything.

Hapscomb pulled out a chair, sat down. He had to do his job. He was so tired but he still had to do his job. Nancy poured him some coffee. "Feels a little bright in here," she said and then she was up, flitting from window to window, pulling the curtains closed. As she busied herself,

Hapscomb explained everything as quickly as he could, did his job like he was supposed to, spoke without slowing. He talked about how he'd arranged to meet with Fox Peterson. About how he'd left Derrick Tupper in charge of the station and drove out to Ryan. How Fox had found God while in prison. How he was born-again. How he'd been reading philosophy. How he wanted to set right his wrongs. "Did you know, Dan, that your sister owes Fox a considerable sum of money? That Fox, in turn, owes that money to someone else? That Fox is only safe on account of his being in prison? Did you know that she is in trouble with some very tough people? Did you ever get the sense that she was desperate?"

Dan's words unfolded slowly, his tongue dry in his mouth, ineffective, but he still managed to talk, express himself; he told Hapscomb about Grace asking him for money, about the notes she'd been leaving him. "Notes, what notes? Let me see them." And so Dan had gotten them, sat and waited while Hapscomb read them, watched the detective's eyes slide from left to right, left to right, left to right, taking it all in, making those connections that cops need to make. Doing their job. "What does this mean?" Hapscomb said, sliding the letter across the table over to Dan, index finger tapping at a line of text. *How come when I tried to tell you about The Worm, you told me I was crazy?* "And this?" *You cannot eat your own tail and disappear into nothingness.* "And this?" *I am going to the river's end.*

"I don't have any idea what any of those things mean. She's crazy. She's a crazy person."

"Robertson," Hapscomb said, "listen to me. I know you're upset. I know you just lost your mother. And I don't want to waste any more time here. So let me level with you." He sat back in his chair, folded his arms. "Despite what I told you earlier, I'm beginning to question your involvement in the homicide of Kenneth Thompkins." It wasn't true, but sometimes, in the name of justice, you had to put the fear in someone to get what you wanted. "I've already got enough to press charges and haul you in." Another lie. But Dan's eyes were wide, his breathing quick and shallow, and Hapscomb knew he just had to keep pushing. He had him. Now he could finally get the answers he wanted. "But I think your sister might know something both you and I don't. Something that Tom Lucas might've known. And that something is somewhere in these letters. In code." He leaned forward, pointed right in Dan's face. "You held onto these letters without telling me. These are important. That's obstruction of justice. Obstructing a criminal investigation." Dan was breathing like crazy now, eyes darting all around Hapscomb's face, looking for something, maybe some inkling that this was a misunderstanding. But he wasn't gonna find it. "And unless you work with me, help me figure out where she might be, well, I'm just gonna have to work with what I've got—and that's you. So talk to me. Think real hard. What do these things mean? Who's The Worm? Where does the river end?"

He let Dan sit and stew for a few seconds. Took note of the deep crease in his brow. Dan was rubbing at his face, his eyes, smoothing his hair, sucking down excess saliva.

He was thinking, thinking hard, searching his memory. Or not quite. Maybe he was making a decision, deciding whether or not to talk, to spill what he knew. And then Dan's eyes were locked onto Hapscomb's. Dan cleared his throat. "She's talking about Bicycle Bob."

"The guy you told me about in the car?"

"Yes. When we were kids, Grace and I, there was an incident."

"An incident?"

Hapscomb felt Nancy standing behind him, just standing there, too close, listening. Dan didn't seem to notice, or at least he didn't seem to care.

"At Silver Creek. We used to play there when we were kids. And then something happened. Something bad. She tried to tell me, I think. A few times. But I never listened. It's like a black spot in my mind. I left her there. In the sewer pipe by the big grate. The one that looks like a huge mouth. I know that much. And you gotta believe me when I tell you this, but I don't know what she's talking about, eating tails and all that, I don't know what that means. She's not well. She's on drugs. She doesn't think clearly— never has. But she mentions Silver Creek in that letter. Like she's obsessed with it. And I've just got this feeling... I've just got this feeling that that's where we need to start looking."

"That's where the river ends," Nancy said, her voice tired, hard as nails. "The grated sewer pipe at the end of the Silver Creek. The runoff from the Thornapple filters through Silver Creek and into the old city sewer. That's the end."

Hapscomb looked at the letter one more time. ...*this is the last day. You will see.* There was no time left. He pushed his chair back from the table, legs scraping against the linoleum, stood up. "Show me how to get to Silver Creek."

They left Nancy behind. Hapscomb told her to make some phone calls, see who was at the station, send someone over to the house, someone who knew the area. There was a body that had to be moved. Send whoever was left out to the city sewer grate. Just in case.

Nighttime wasn't far off. It was already four in the afternoon. Hapscomb grabbed a Maglite out of his car and they were off.

It was a walk through the woods, a trek through the kingdom of Dan's childhood, behind the Robertson house, through the ice-covered fields, dead trees here and there, over a few gurgling streams, the woods, blue jays and cardinals zipping from tree to tree, the dead and bare trees, up a hill around a hill, the sun sinking in the sky, changing colors, orange bleeding to red fading to yellow to white, the nighttime sky setting in, like always, but somehow ominous, the crunch of the snow beneath their boots, the flakes falling fat like feathers after a pillow fight, just careless kids bopping each other over the head with their pillows, no thought of hurting one another, no malice, just play, kid's stuff, this kingdom of kids.

They came to the creek, a trench dug into the ground, its walls lined with green-rotted planks of wood, mossy where they met the mud, its bed dried up and frozen. "We just follow this to the end," Dan said, bending his knees, putting a gloved hand on the lip of the creek's wall, supporting himself, before dropping in. Hapscomb followed. They stood there. Two grown men. "It's about fifteen minutes from here," Dan said.

Hapscomb looked up into the sky. It was getting dark. And fast. The pistol felt heavy on his hip.

Dan seemed lost in a world of his own. They continued on, following the creek bed. Following it to its end.

The grate was massive, ten-feet tall and just as wide, a black gaping maw carved into a concrete wall jutting out from the slope of a low hill. Steel bars were spaced evenly, a foot or so apart, across its opening. It emerged out of the wilderness like an afterthought, the way man-made things often do. An ugliness. The head of a beast ripping up through the ground, its sides covered in the brown and brittle threads of ivy, wrapped in the roots of the trees that had grown above it, roots like the tendrils of giant squids, wrapping themselves around the hull of a ship. Or, at least, this is the way Dan had always seen it, when he was a child, when his imagination had been able to run free. He had always seen this thing as the head of a giant buried beast, its mouth open wide in a scream, its guts the system of pipes burrowing through the underground, stinking and limitless.

A wind blew through the trees like a wolf howl, piercing, lonesome, snowflakes twirling through the air, nothing sticking. The nighttime sky had frozen over dark and Hapscomb clicked on the Maglite, aimed its broadening beam into the sewer's maw, the light finding no register in the blackness as he swept it from side to side, gleaming off the steel bars, disappearing again into the blackness.

"It's deep," Hapscomb said.

"Goes back a long ways," Dan said. "Connects the whole goddamn town to what used to be an old settlement. All that was left to rot years ago. And this is what's left. It's a ruins."

The moon was everywhere, where they stood in that creek bed, the smooth hills rolling all around them like the rumpled sheets of a quiet, unmade bed, frosted in the dull blue winter moonlight.

How he missed his bed. He felt out-of-body. The tiredness that Dan just couldn't shake from these last three days, from this long life, welled up in him like a sigh, exited his body in a tattered cloud of breath. And when he watched that breath disappear into the air he knew that he was ready for whatever awaited him, that every action he'd ever made had led him here, to this sewer, to this darkness.

A low noise like a mewling leaked from the pipe's blackness, both near and far at the same time, an echo in a dream, the whimpering of an injured animal. And by the time Dan had finished saying *Did you hear that?* Hapscomb had his gun out, arm locked in place, gun held before his face, Maglite in his other hand, illuminating what could be the path of a bullet. There it was again, the mewling, trickling from the darkness, carried away by the wind, just barely discernible but there, yes, definitely there.

The snow squished beneath Dan's boot as he shifted his weight. Then, and this time louder, another whimper, another cry. Hapscomb lowered the gun and the light, motioned to Dan to stay put, took a few slow steps forward.

But Dan couldn't stay put, not when he'd come this far. He took a step, snow crunching. Hapscomb spun around, furious, gestured again to stay put. Dan shook his head. Mouthed "No." The two men locked eyes, stalemate.

"What are you gonna do?" Dan whispered. "It's my sister."

Hapscomb shook his head, said as quietly as he could, enunciating every single shape of each word, "Too dangerous." Then, "Don't be stupid."

And that was it. Hapscomb turned and slid through the bars, disappeared into the dark.

Fuck him, Dan thought, following, staying just far enough behind. The bars were closer together than Dan remembered, or no, that was stupid, he'd just grown so much bigger, and he had to suck in his stomach to slide between them.

Glutted with decay, a mineral-rich stench, the air in the sewer was stagnant, cold, tomb-like. Dan's careful footsteps fell as soft clicks in the thinly frozen bed of silt. He listened, heard Hapscomb some ten or twelve feet in front of him. He let the sounds guide him through the dark.

And then he saw the light click on, its beam visible in the air's thickness, hitting him square in the eyes. Dan moved toward the light, was about to say something when that noise, that mewling, so much louder this time, made him stop.

Hapscomb turned around, moving quickly, and Dan followed, the mewling growing louder, louder. They covered fifty yards. A hundred. The concrete cylinder continued on in a straight line. Dan heard a voice he recognized. Grace's voice.

She was yelling, her voice distorted by the echo, overlapping itself in stony waves. She was close, just up ahead, around a sharp turn.

Dan heard Hapscomb's breathing, loud, a rasp. He saw a flash of Bicycle Bob's face, the Demon makeup, the mouth drooling blood, in his memory. Those hideous yellow teeth all thin and black pockets. This was where it had happened.

The knife biting into his shoulder. *My God, what had happened?* He could still feel its coldness in his skin. The memory of it in his muscle. It came back to him then, strong, like a warning.

It wasn't too far now. He was getting close to something inside himself.

They stopped moving, Hapscomb killed the light, whispered in Dan's ear to turn around, to get out, but Dan wouldn't listen, couldn't stand the thought of his sister lost in here, in the darkness, alone and six years old and crying. They stood still, listening, staring at one another, Hapscomb motioning to Dan to turn around, Dan shaking his head in refusal.

Grace was ranting, her words coming out jagged and uneven, like she was crying as she spoke, hiccupping pockets of confused language. "Why are you looking at me like that? Don't you get it? Life is hard and pointless. Can't you see that this is a gift I'm giving you?" More hiccups, wailing. The mewling. Whoever she was talking to was mewling, begging, voice muffled, gagged.

Dan's hands shook, were shaking, a flash flood of a child's fear, Bicycle Bob.

Hapscomb tightened his grip on the gun, the body of the Maglite. *Now is not the time to be a coward*, he thought. He turned the corner, flicked on the light, gun out. "Police." Dan barely had time to follow him, almost swallowed whole by the dark.

A rush of movement. Confusion and sound. The beam of the light swung everywhere, picking out details. Hapscomb was yelling, "Put your hands up where I can see them. Let me see your hands. Drop the gun." And then the light hit Grace's pale face. She was there, like a phantom, all of them cramped together, there, in the darkness, so close together. Grace was just a floating face in the dark, pink and pale and trembling, her hair bent and crooked and lit up red like sun flares. The light was all over the place, Hapscomb shining here, there, trying to figure out was going on. It was all happening too quickly. There was too much to take in. Grace yelling *what the fuck what the fuck what the fuck*. There was a body on an old filthy mattress, the girl, the girl from Fox's cabin, her hands bound behind her back, face turned to the wall, ponytail stained with mud. The gleam of a gun, a pistol, in her hands. "Is she dead?" Dan yelled. "Drop the weapon," Hapscomb yelled. *What the fuck what the fuck what the fuck.* And then another body. Kenneth Jr. On his knees, hands behind his back, mouth gagged with a white strip of cloth. Still very much alive, nostrils flaring like crazy. The concave walls of the tunnel were covered in graffiti: inverted crosses, pentagrams, illegible scrawl. All of these details came through in pieces, fragments, out of order.

Dan screamed, trying to make his voice heard above the other voices. "What did you do? Jesus God, what did you do?"

And then Hapscomb's voice was the loudest and he said, "Drop the gun or I'm going to shoot. Drop the gun."

And then Grace's voice was the loudest and she said, "This isn't the way it happens. This isn't what happens."

And then Dan's voice was the loudest again and he said, "Don't shoot her." And then, "Jesus God, Grace, what did you do?" Or at least he thought he said that.

Grace let the gun—a heavy revolver—drop from her hand. It fell to the ground with a thud. That sound was followed by the loudest kind of silence, and then the sound of Kenneth Jr.'s whimpering, his gagged pleading, quieting down, dropping off. It took a few seconds for the tunnel to clear itself of the echo of voices.

"This is the only way," Grace said.

"You killed that girl, didn't you?" Dan said.

"Dan, shut up," Hapscomb said, taking another step closer to Grace, keeping the light trained square on her face.

"How could you do that?" Dan said, ignoring Hapscomb, his voice rising.

"The girl doesn't live," Grace said. "She wasn't pure."

"Both of you shut up," Hapscomb said. "Grace, do not go near that gun. Stay where you are. Do not move, don't do anything. I will shoot. Good. Stay where you are." He took shuffling side-steps, getting closer to the gun Grace had dropped.

"This is all your fault, Dan," Grace said.

"Me? You killed that girl. You killed a girl. How is that my fault?"

"I said shut the fuck up," Hapscomb said, "both of you shut the fuck up."

The kid was going nuts, making noise, thrashing around on the ground, his cries and sobs muffled by the gag.

Grace had her hands over her ears. She shook her head back and forth. *"Shut the fuck up shut the fuck up shut the fuck up."*

"Grace," Hapscomb said, but didn't get to finish what he was going to say.

The detective took another step forward, almost within arm's reach of Grace.

Dan saw, on the wall behind Grace, in the light, a massive, sprawling spray-painted mural covering the entire tunnel, everything in view. It showed some sort of monster, painted in lumpy blacks and greens, its twisted mouth open filled with gleaming silver spikes, another mouth inside its mouth, turned sideways like a vagina, its lips glistening blood. The monster was floating in outer space, amongst burning stars and brightly colored planets, like it was coming forward through a tear in space, from some unknown dimension, half in, half out. And the words in blocky white letters beneath it, "The Bornless One." Dan took just enough time to look at the mural to realize that he'd let his thoughts get away from him.

What happened next only took a few seconds, and in the dark, outside of the Maglite's illumination, was forever lost. It was only sound. The scuff of Grace's sneakers as she lunged for the pistol she'd dropped. Kenneth Jr.'s muffled moans. The concussion of Hapscomb's gun going off. The ping of its bullet—missing Grace—as it struck the wall. The lung-singing stink of spent gunpowder, everywhere like a fog. The second, third, and fourth pings as the bullet ricocheted, zipping around the sewer pipe like an insect, shedding small bursts of orange sparks before lodging itself, like a white hot hornet's sting, in the meat of Dan's thigh. Dan's scream. The second concussion of a handgun firing, only this time, it was Grace who pulled the trigger, and there was no ricocheting bullet.

Warm blood filled Dan's ear canals, crawled sticky down his neck. His leg was numb.

Hapscomb shined the beam of the Maglite on Grace's body lying facedown in the mud. Dan was able to see what had happened, how the back of his sister's head had bloomed a new hole. She'd eaten a bullet, given herself the gift of eternal black, the peace she'd always wanted.

The ringing in Dan's ears was like a thousand bicycle bells jingling away in same dark memory, the sound pulsing to the beat of the dull ache in his thigh where the bullet hit, as steady and rhythmic as a heartbeat, the fiery sting of the scar on his shoulder, fading to a cold itch, and then disappearing altogether.

~

If Hapscomb tried to say anything, tried to console him, he never heard it.

The light moved across the tunnel and, for just a second, Dan caught a glimpse of his sister's blood, thick and oozing black, as it pooled, fanning outward beneath her body, mixing into that pathetic, stream of silt, those corrosive waters running through that sewer pipe.

And those were the same waters, Dan knew, that would, in the springtime, be fed by the creek as it thrashed back to life.

The same waters that would make their way to the treatment facility in Forest Hills.

Those same waters that would, eventually—because that was the lay of the land—make their way back to the Thornapple River. Where they would then be lost.

The boy, Kenneth Jr., confessed to his role in his father's murder immediately after Hapscomb brought him into the station. It was like he always said, sometimes you have to put the fear in someone to get what you want. The kid was all shaken up from what he'd seen happen to his sister. Who could blame him? But Hapscomb wasn't there to comfort him. The boy didn't deserve it, anyway. He was there to explain the significance of Kenneth Jr.'s crimes. The pre-meditated murder of his father. Distribution of a controlled substance. Those two were just the beginning. Things would get really messy once they broke out the red tape.

It wasn't a huge surprise to learn that the gun Grace Robertson had used to blow her head off was a .357 Magnum, registered to one Thomas Lucas.

Corroborating statements made by William Peterson effectively closed the case:

"Those fucking kids stole it out the back of his truck one night when we were at Rose's. Look, I'm not gonna lie to you. Tom had invested money in Grace's meth operation, was backing those kids, taking a percentage of what they sold—even pushing some of it himself. Fox knew about it, I think. But Tom got burned when Grace ran into money problems. He got mouthy. Kenneth's kids took the gun, I guess, because it was the only way they could get one. Maybe if they thought Tom was implicated in something they'd done, he wouldn't be able to go blabbing about nothing. Or maybe they just wanted to fuck him over. It was all Grace's idea—that I know for sure. She sent Tom a note the day after his gun disappeared, after Kenneth Sr. wound up dead, and told him to go to her brother and bring him out to the body, that Dan would know what to do. She said Dan would bury him secret in the graveyard. Get rid of the Jeep. She said Dan owed her a favor and there'd be no fuss. No questions asked. 'Course, once we actually got him out there, we realized that Grace was full of shit and that Dan was clueless—and that just made shit a whole hell of a lot more complicated, you ask me. We knew we were fucked, but Tom wouldn't accept it. I think she just wanted to fuck her brother over, too. Scare him. That was Grace for you. Always fucking up everyone's shit."

Hapscomb and Peterson talked for a little while. Just about things. And that's when Bill mentioned the story of Bicycle Bob. The legend. What had happened down there at Silver Creek. How Grace had been abducted as a child, raped. And her child's mind had put together the legend of The Worm because, who knows, she probably had no other way of coping with her pain.

So she repressed what happened, fed her fears, fed her belief in the Worm. Allowed that belief to mix with her real life, and the lives of others.

"Dan said you and him saw Bicycle Bob once, out in the woods, when you were kids."

Bill nodded. "That's right," he said. "But Dan got all the details wrong."

"How do you mean?"

"He said Bicycle Bob looked like Gene Simmons from KISS. All that stupid makeup and everything. But he didn't. He didn't look like that at all."

"What did he look like?"

Bill sighed, titled his head back—the gesture of a helpless man asking for something from the heavens. His neck strained with the words before he began speaking them.

"He looked just like my uncle, my dad's brother. Uncle Roland." A big, big sigh. And then his eyes were locked on Hapscomb's. His voice held something in it, some hurt that was locked down deep somewhere. "Roland was a bad dude."

Hapscomb went for the direct question, the question he'd been wanting to ask each and every person who'd mentioned Bicycle Bob. "Was he real? Was Bob actually real?"

"He was real."

"Was it actually your uncle out there that night?"

"No."

"How do you know? How can you be sure?"

"Because Roland was in prison serving a life sentence for doing some things I'd rather not mention at the moment. There's no way it was him. No way it could have been. Ever." And then Bill clammed up tight. Didn't matter what Hapscomb said, what questions he asked, Bill just stopped talking.

Deep down, Hapscomb knew that it was the closest he was ever going to get to the truth about Bob, whoever or whatever it was.

Things fell into place after that.

In a few weeks, Derrick Tupper, newly stripped of his badge, would go before the judge on charges of Aiding and Abetting.

Samuel Veen was still on the run somewhere. But guys like him never got too far before they were found. They weren't clever enough. Didn't have the motivation.

Fox Peterson would be released in a few days, on parole, from the Ryan Correctional Facility.

Crimes like this sort of had a way of working themselves out. When you've got several people all struggling against each other, each trying to protect themselves and no one else, well, things tend to get real messy real fast and then, once the dust clears, you can see the truth pretty plainly.

Things always work themselves out if they're meant to. It's all a matter of looking at a situation with the right kind of eyes. Otherwise you might miss something important. And that's what it's all about. The way you look at things. What they might mean to you.

And this crime seemed simple enough to Hapscomb, when he thought about it all, when he read through his reports. All the pieces seemed to fit together. As long as he ignored all the things that didn't make so much sense: the weird darkness that seemed to haunt these people, the conflicting versions of Bicycle Bob. But none of that mattered, not to him, because come tomorrow he would leave Ardor behind, go back to real life, and it made him so thankful to realize this he actually muttered a prayer, something he hadn't done since childhood, since he was a boy, lying in the darkness of bedtime, scared to go to sleep for fear of not waking.

Hapscomb watched a small Bobcat excavator pull up great rips of earth, its motor rattling in the cold morning air.

It was a great gray day, the overcast sky plated silver, blustery. But the snow was melting, and the ground was showing hints of deep green. Michigan would be beautiful again soon. The weather would wane, as it always did, and always would.

Five people were buried in Ardor's tiny cemetery that morning: Kenneth Thompkins and his daughter Kendra, Tom Lucas, Bessie Robertson and Grace Robertson.

It was more work than the Bobcat had seen in months, more excitement than the little town could handle. Every available seat at each funeral service was filled. There were even news cameras. In all the time he'd spent in Ardor, Hapscomb hadn't seen half this many people. And now here they all were—in one place—dressed in their Sunday best, people whose names he'd never heard mentioned. The rumors had gotten out of control almost immediately, turned into the stuff of legend—but of course, none of the rumors were half as bad as the truth.

As Dan's mother's eulogy was being given, the priest's booming voice half lost to the wind, half filled with rage, rage for God once again taking one of the few, one of the good, rage for the helplessness of the meek, we poor and wanting worms, Nancy whispered to herself, "That play is the tragedy 'Man,' and its hero the Conqueror Worm," without thinking and then Dan's hand was gripping her just above the elbow, his face was streaming tears and he was saying, *What was that where did you hear that why did you say that.*

The massive bonfire lit up the clearing in the woods a bright, burning yellow, the fire raging the only noise, drowning everything else out, the flames licking at the dark like whips. Embers broke free of the fire, dozens every second, drifting into the sky, blinking out of existence like so many evil eyes.

In the far reaches of the light, the naked trees looked pale, sickly, partially consumed by the limitless night beyond.

Heavy chains were nailed high in the trees, hanging slack, holding small bloodstained cages filled with live chickens, frantic and fluttering their wings. Another, larger cage held a fully-grown goat, lying down, legs tucked beneath its body. The goat was silent, watchful.

And all around the fire, dozens of men and women in their winter jackets, knit caps over their heads, some standing, others kneeling, bowed their heads to the ground, all facing the flames. The yellow flash of lighters here and there, illuminating faces in the dark, shining eyes, the curve of a nose, the meth catching the flame and burning cherry-hot. Great clouds of the holy smoke everywhere.

Lawrence Newbert stood shirtless some ten feet away from the bonfire, his giant goat-skull tattoo lit up and flickering in the light on his sweating skin. He wore a black ski mask. From far away, he looked like he had no head at all, swallowed by the black. He raised his arms to the sky and anyone left standing dropped to their knees. Everyone on their knees.

A noise like a growl, Teddy emerging from behind his brother, also shirtless, also raising his arms to the sky, the brothers growling like junkyard dogs. Everyone rose to their feet, formed a line, and marched into the darkness, following the brothers into the deep woods. In the distance, rising above the tree line, stood the sharp angle of a black barn, the lines of its roof gleaming in the moonlight, a black weathervane at its apex shaped into a Leviathan Cross.

Brother Lawrence began his sermon from behind the stone altar at the head of the barn. Chains hung from the rafters, candelabra twirling at their end, dripping wax into the dirt below. The pews, merely stacks of long wood boards, were filled with the faithful, with the takers of the holy smoke.

"By the end of the twentieth century," Brother Lawrence said, "all logging and manufacturing activity along the banks of our Thornapple River had ceased. The Flour Mill, the Saw Mill—those things now exist as little more than photographs in some of the tourist-trap gift shops in town.

"But the Thornapple, that's the vein that pumped blood into the land. We've buried our dead in these grounds, even as recently as our youngest, Sweet Baby Clayton."

Dozens of "Amens" muttered among the faithful.

"It is an ugly river, the Thornapple," Brother Lawrence continued, "a river of muddy waters, a river that cuts through terrible woods. And they say, in some places, where the river has wormed its way through the thickest throngs of trees, where its waters run the deepest, providing hatching grounds for blood-sucking bugs and witch toads, the flesh form of the demon prince Baal, they say that you can hear laugher echoing back and forth, from one embankment to the other.

"I've heard some people say that this laughter, it's the soul of Bicycle Bob, the child rapist, lord of The Worm, out there living amongst the trees like the evil bornless spirit. And I've heard others say that it's the spirit of the woods itself. I don't believe in man's petty creations, ghosts, or Indian burial grounds, or anything like that. No. There is a Lord of Lords. And he is the creator. And some places, some of the places that bear his mark, are just bad. Some places are black to their core, were never meant to be settled, civilized, tread by the feet of men's industry.

"Those of us who feel this way, those of you who join me here tonight to worship, who believe that these woods are something more than just trees, something alive, fed by the waters of that terrible river, we channel our thoughts like a prayer, an offering to the Bornless One, an appeal, concession to his poverty. And we repeat this prayer over and over and over again."

The faithful rose from their seats. And everyone listened as Brother Lawrence gave his prayer, his voice echoing through the barn with great force and will.

Thee I invoke: the Bornless One.
Thou that didst create the Earth and the Heavens,
Thou that didst create the Night and the Day,

Thou that didst create the Darkness and the Light,

Thou art the Bornless One: Whom no man hath seen at any time,

Thou hast distinguished between the just and the unjust.

Thou didst make the female and the male.

Thou didst produce the seed and the fruit.

Thou didst form men to love one another, and to hate one another.

Brother Lawrence extended his arm and, with two fingers, marked the five points of the inverted star.

"My brothers and sisters, we shall repeat our appeal to the Bornless One. Say it with me now."

DAVID PEAK is the author of *Surface Tension* and *Glowing in the Dark*.

CPSIA information can be obtained
at www.ICGtesting.com
Printed in the USA
BVHW030959210223
658926BV00008B/55